OUT FROM BONEVILLE

BY JEFF SMITH
WITH COLOR BY STEVE HAMAKER

An Imprint of

SCHOLASTIC

This book is for Vijaya

Library of Congress Cataloging-in-Publication Data is available.
ISBN-13: 978-0-439-70623-0 – ISBN-10: 0-439-70623-8 (hardcover)
ISBN 0-439-70640-8 (paperback)

ACKNOWLEDGMENTS
Harvestar Family Crest designed by Charles Vess
Map of *The Valley* by Mark Crilley

40 39 38 37 36 35 34 33 32   17 18 19
First Scholastic edition, February 2005
Book design by David Saylor
Printed in Malaysia 108

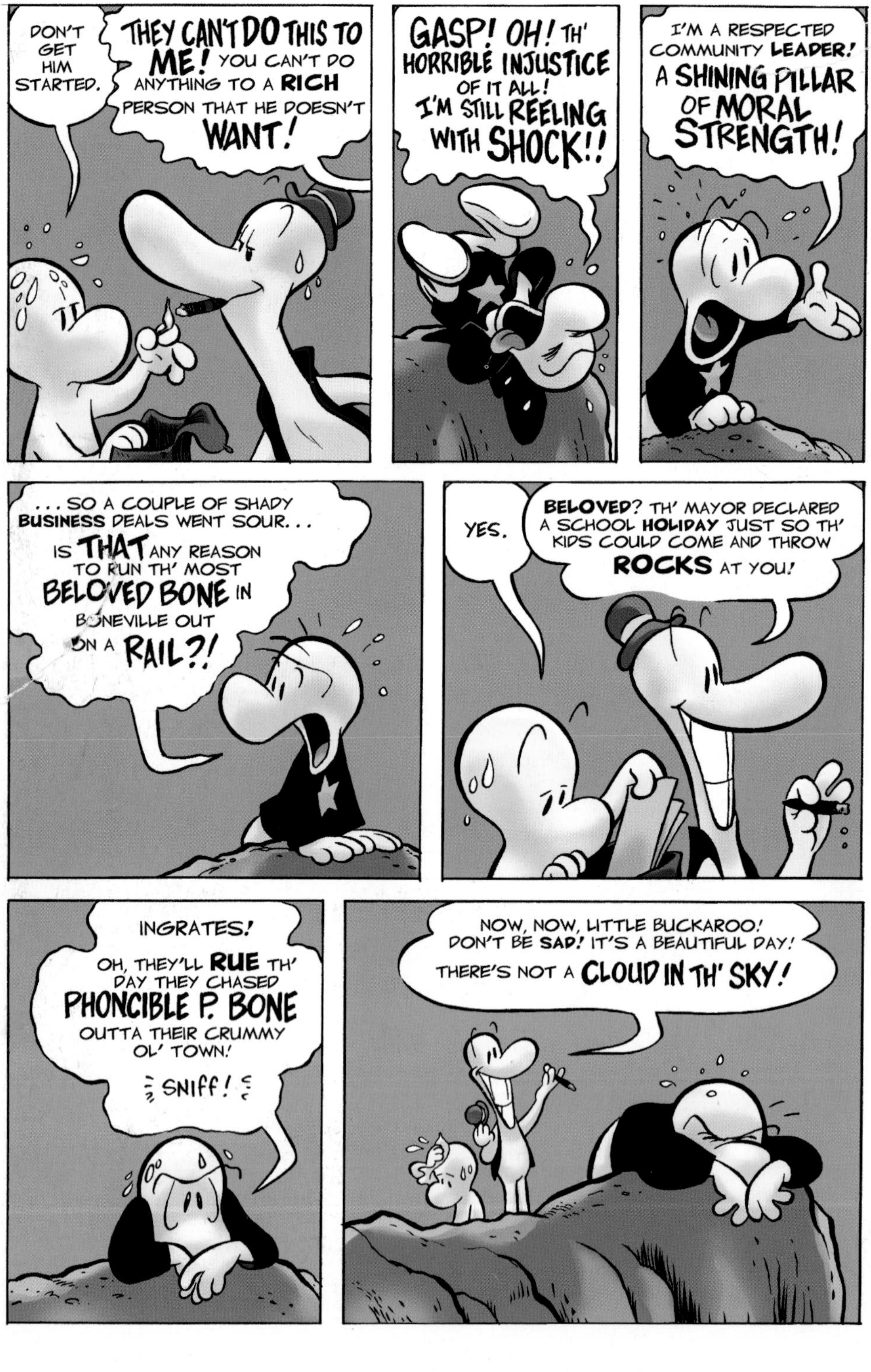
DON'T GET HIM STARTED.
THEY CAN'T DO THIS TO ME! YOU CAN'T DO ANYTHING TO A RICH PERSON THAT HE DOESN'T WANT!
GASP! OH! TH' HORRIBLE INJUSTICE OF IT ALL! I'M STILL REELING WITH SHOCK!!
I'M A RESPECTED COMMUNITY LEADER! A SHINING PILLAR OF MORAL STRENGTH!
. . . SO A COUPLE OF SHADY BUSINESS DEALS WENT SOUR. . . IS THAT ANY REASON TO RUN TH' MOST BELOVED BONE IN BONEVILLE OUT ON A RAIL?!
YES.
BELOVED? TH' MAYOR DECLARED A SCHOOL HOLIDAY JUST SO TH' KIDS COULD COME AND THROW ROCKS AT YOU!
INGRATES! OH, THEY'LL RUE TH' DAY THEY CHASED PHONCIBLE P. BONE OUTTA THEIR CRUMMY OL' TOWN!
SNIFF!
NOW, NOW, LITTLE BUCKAROO! DON'T BE SAD! IT'S A BEAUTIFUL DAY! THERE'S NOT A CLOUD IN TH' SKY!

THE MAP

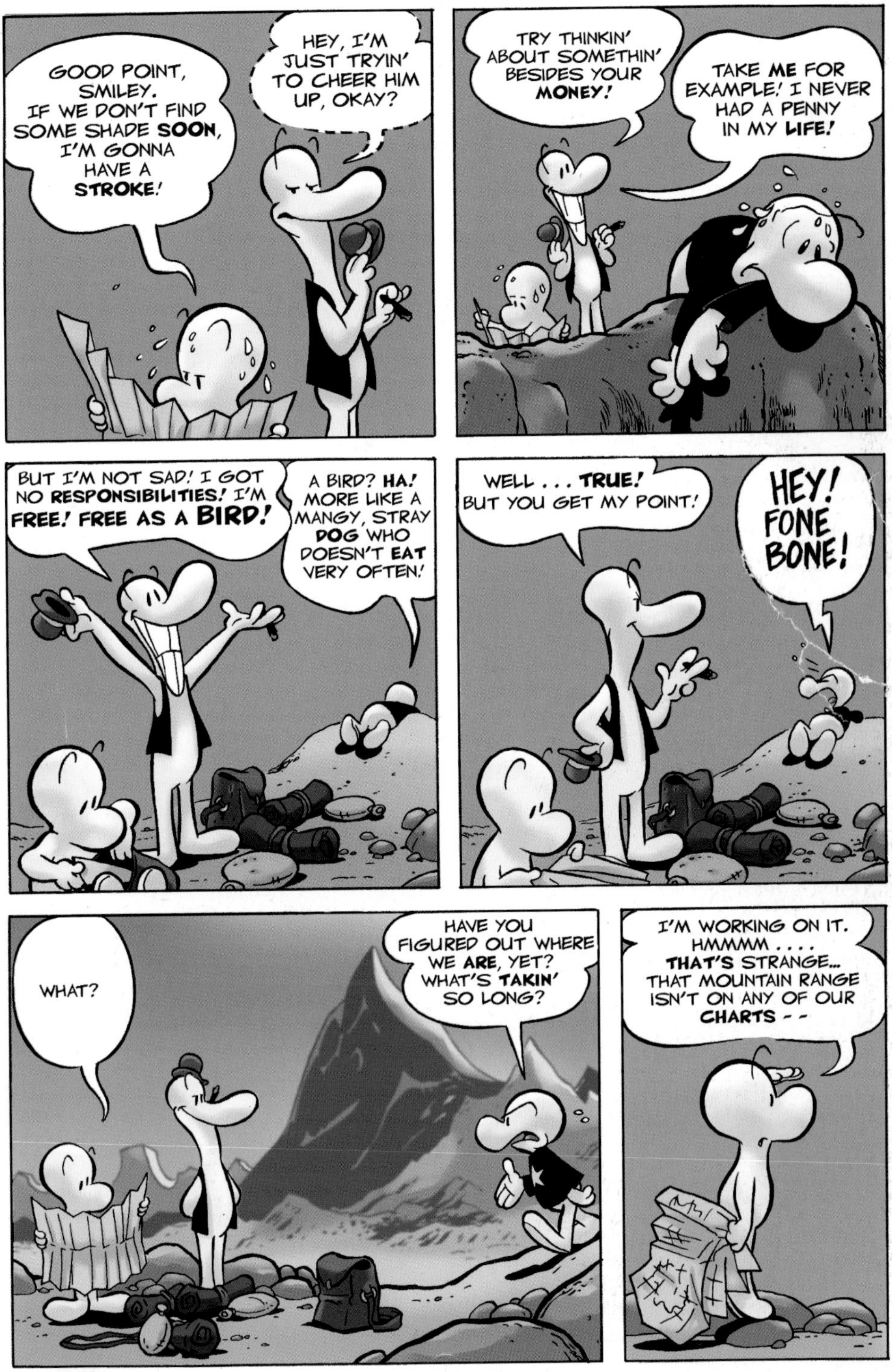
GOOD POINT, SMILEY. IF WE DON'T FIND SOME SHADE SOON, I'M GONNA HAVE A STROKE!
HEY, I'M JUST TRYIN' TO CHEER HIM UP, OKAY?
TRY THINKIN' ABOUT SOMETHIN' BESIDES YOUR MONEY!
TAKE ME FOR EXAMPLE! I NEVER HAD A PENNY IN MY LIFE!
BUT I'M NOT SAD! I GOT NO RESPONSIBILITIES! I'M FREE! FREE AS A BIRD!
A BIRD? HA! MORE LIKE A MANGY, STRAY DOG WHO DOESN'T EAT VERY OFTEN!
WELL . . . TRUE! BUT YOU GET MY POINT!
HEY! FONE BONE!
WHAT?
HAVE YOU FIGURED OUT WHERE WE ARE, YET? WHAT'S TAKIN' SO LONG?
I'M WORKING ON IT. HMMMM . . . . THAT'S STRANGE... THAT MOUNTAIN RANGE ISN'T ON ANY OF OUR CHARTS - -

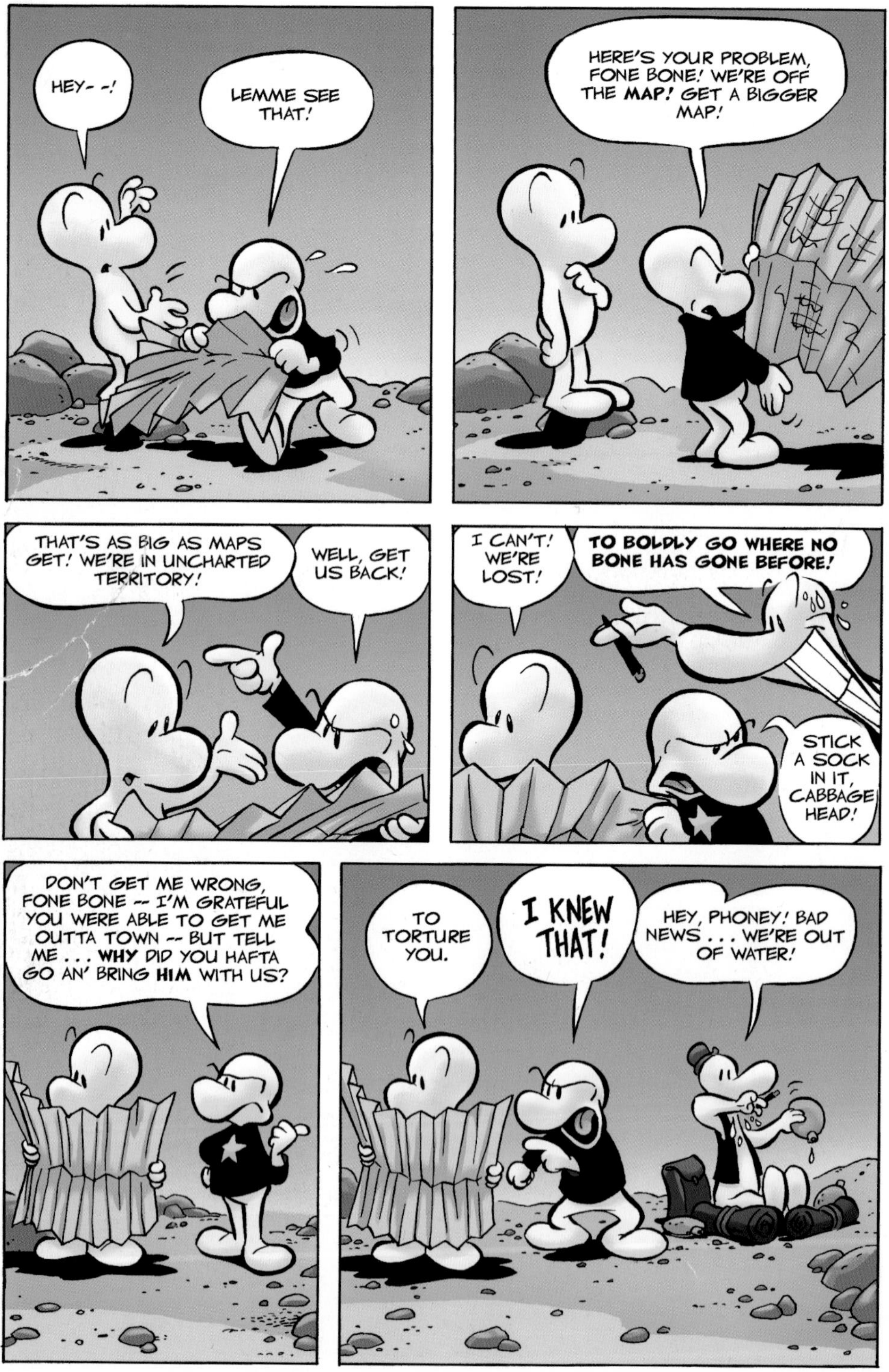
HEY- -!
LEMME SEE THAT!
HERE'S YOUR PROBLEM, FONE BONE! WE'RE OFF THE MAP! GET A BIGGER MAP!
THAT'S AS BIG AS MAPS GET! WE'RE IN UNCHARTED TERRITORY!
WELL, GET US BACK!
I CAN'T! WE'RE LOST!
TO BOLDLY GO WHERE NO BONE HAS GONE BEFORE!
STICK A SOCK IN IT, CABBAGE HEAD!
DON'T GET ME WRONG, FONE BONE -- I'M GRATEFUL YOU WERE ABLE TO GET ME OUTTA TOWN -- BUT TELL ME . . . WHY DID YOU HAFTA GO AN' BRING HIM WITH US?
TO TORTURE YOU.
I KNEW THAT!
HEY, PHONEY! BAD NEWS . . . WE'RE OUT OF WATER!

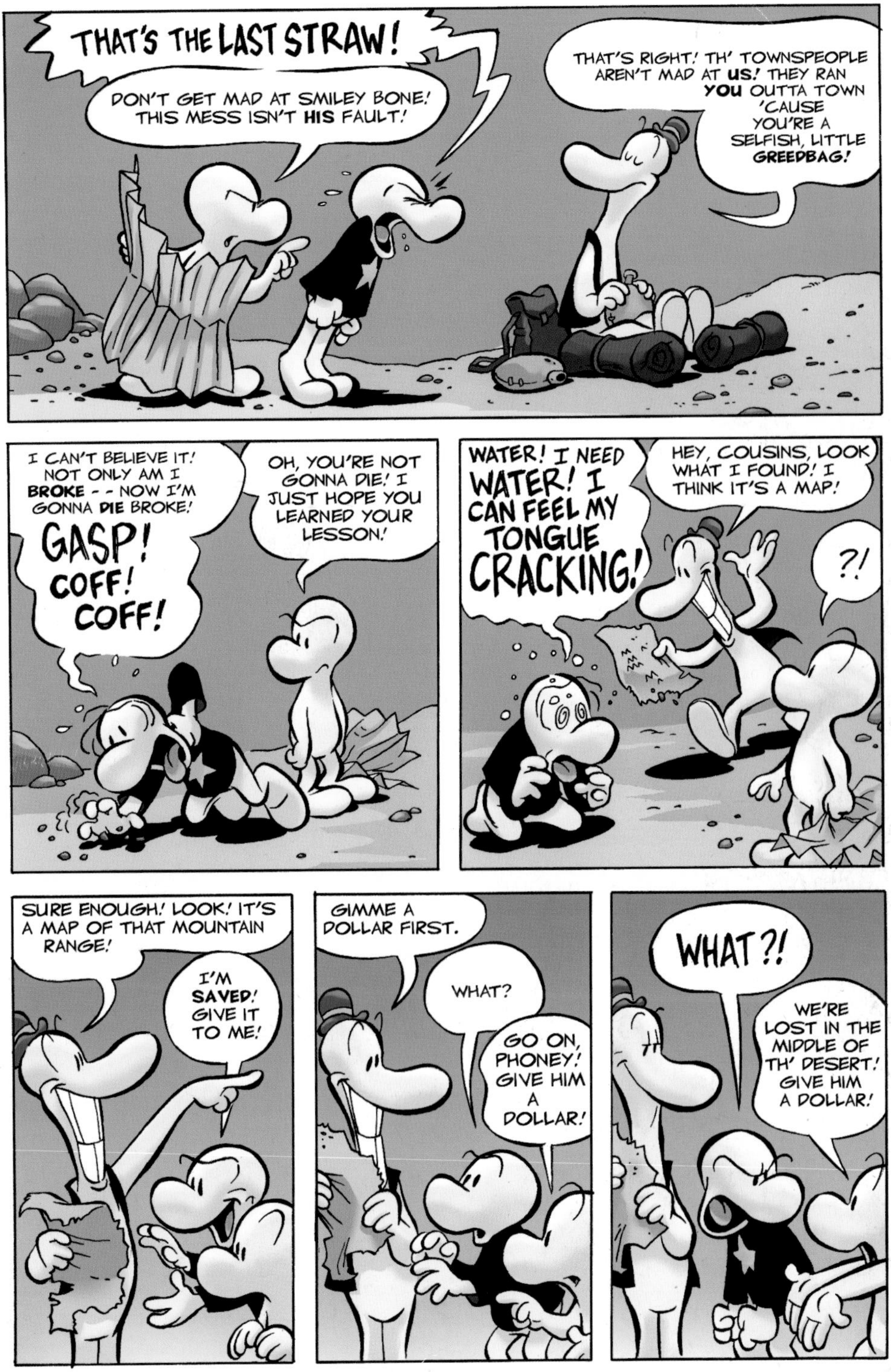
THAT'S THE LAST STRAW!
DON'T GET MAD AT SMILEY BONE! THIS MESS ISN'T HIS FAULT!
THAT'S RIGHT! TH' TOWNSPEOPLE AREN'T MAD AT US! THEY RAN YOU OUTTA TOWN 'CAUSE YOU'RE A SELFISH, LITTLE GREEDBAG!
I CAN'T BELIEVE IT! NOT ONLY AM I BROKE - - NOW I'M GONNA DIE BROKE!
GASP! COFF! COFF!
OH, YOU'RE NOT GONNA DIE! I JUST HOPE YOU LEARNED YOUR LESSON!
WATER! I NEED WATER! I CAN FEEL MY TONGUE CRACKING!
HEY, COUSINS, LOOK WHAT I FOUND! I THINK IT'S A MAP!
?!
SURE ENOUGH! LOOK! IT'S A MAP OF THAT MOUNTAIN RANGE!
I'M SAVED! GIVE IT TO ME!
GIMME A DOLLAR FIRST.
WHAT?
GO ON, PHONEY! GIVE HIM A DOLLAR!
WHAT?!
WE'RE LOST IN THE MIDDLE OF TH' DESERT! GIVE HIM A DOLLAR!

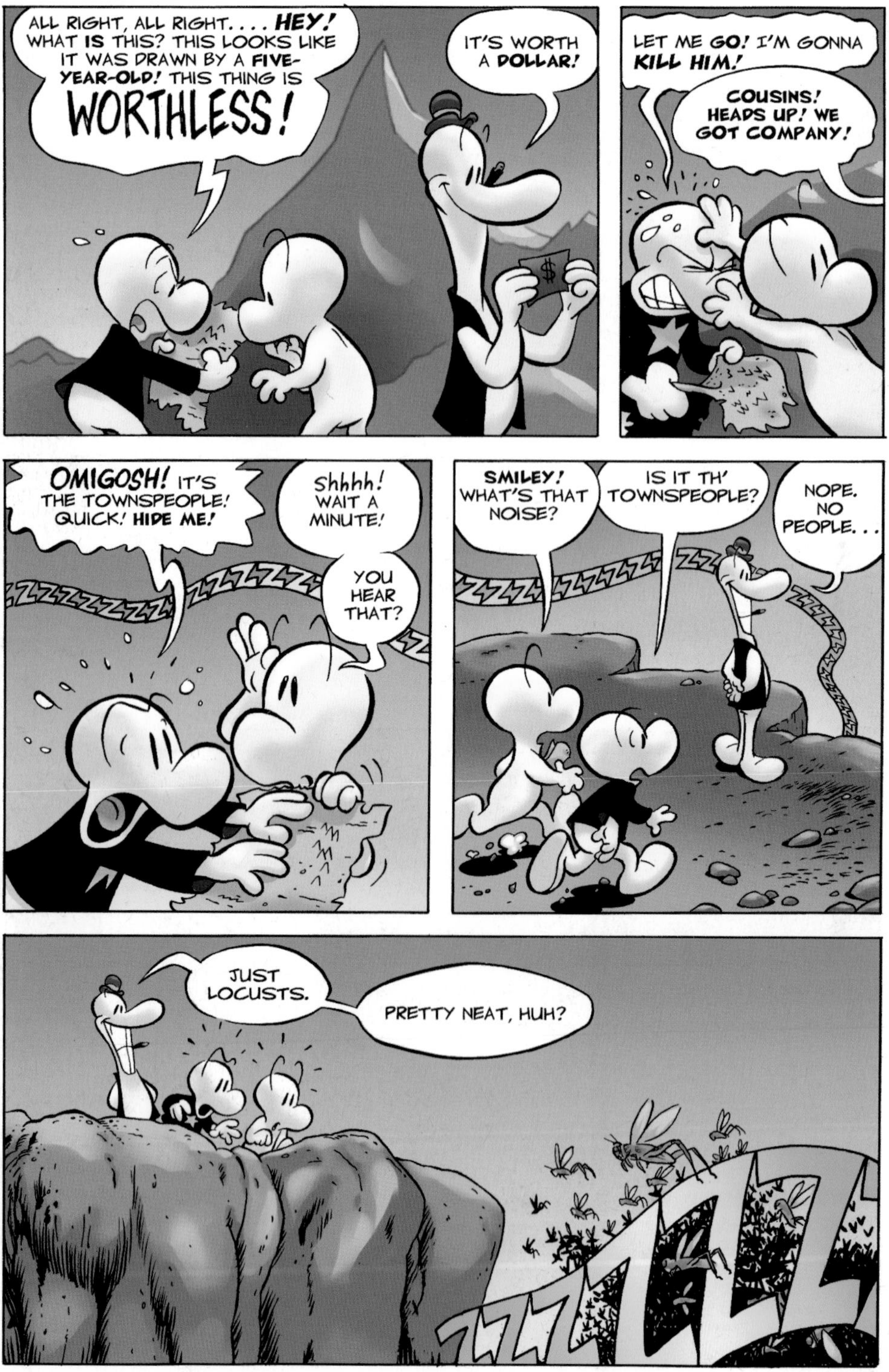
ALL RIGHT, ALL RIGHT. . . . HEY! WHAT IS THIS? THIS LOOKS LIKE IT WAS DRAWN BY A FIVE-YEAR-OLD! THIS THING IS WORTHLESS!
IT'S WORTH A DOLLAR!
LET ME GO! I'M GONNA KILL HIM!
COUSINS! HEADS UP! WE GOT COMPANY!
OMIGOSH! IT'S THE TOWNSPEOPLE! QUICK! HIDE ME!
Shhhh! WAIT A MINUTE!
YOU HEAR THAT?
SMILEY! WHAT'S THAT NOISE?
IS IT TH' TOWNSPEOPLE?
NOPE. NO PEOPLE. . .
JUST LOCUSTS.
PRETTY NEAT, HUH?

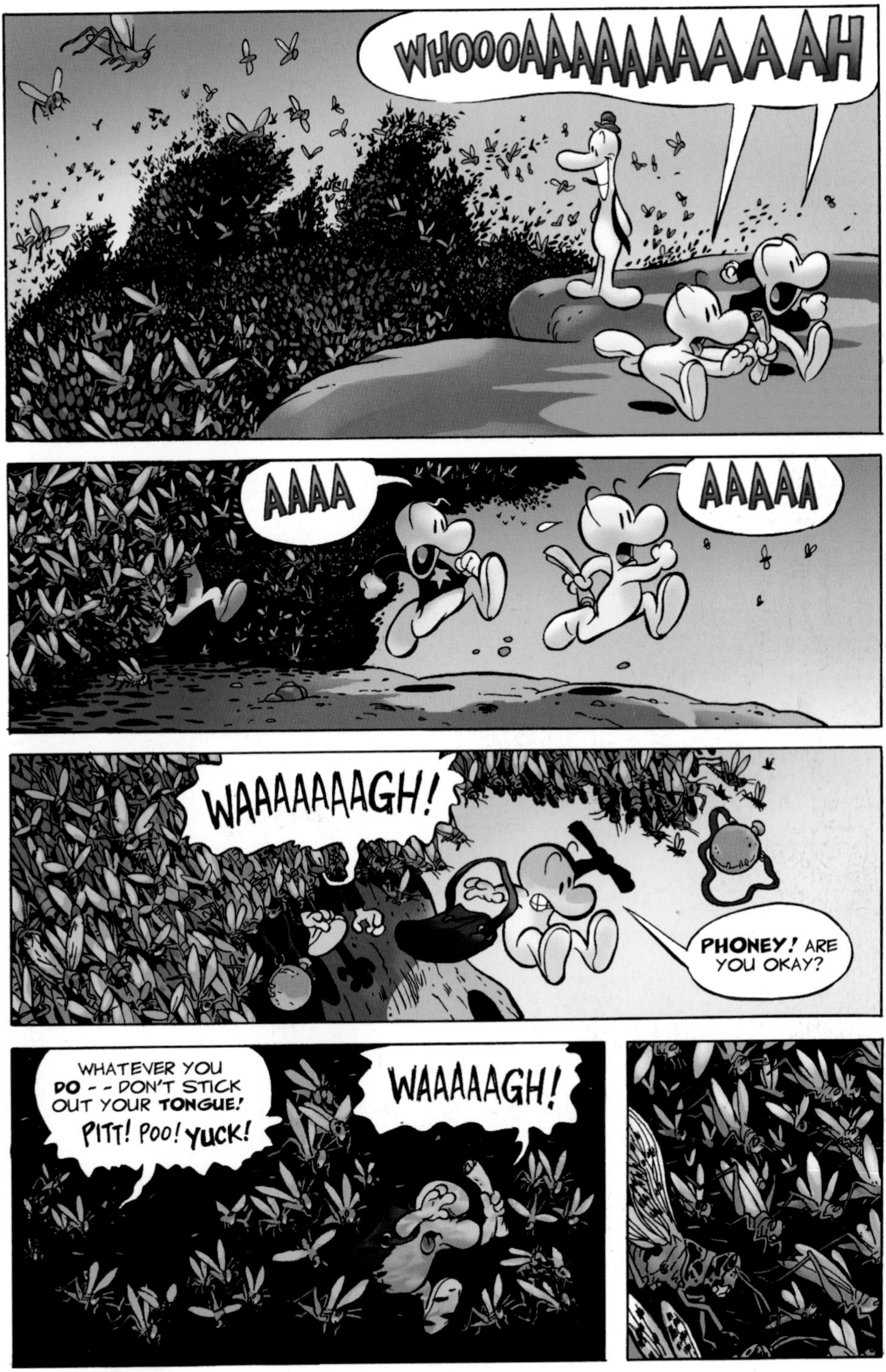
WHOOOAAAAAAAAAAAH
AAAA
AAAAA
WAAAAAAAGH!
PHONEY! ARE YOU OKAY?
WHATEVER YOU DO - - DON'T STICK OUT YOUR TONGUE! PITT! POO! YUCK!
WAAAAAGH!

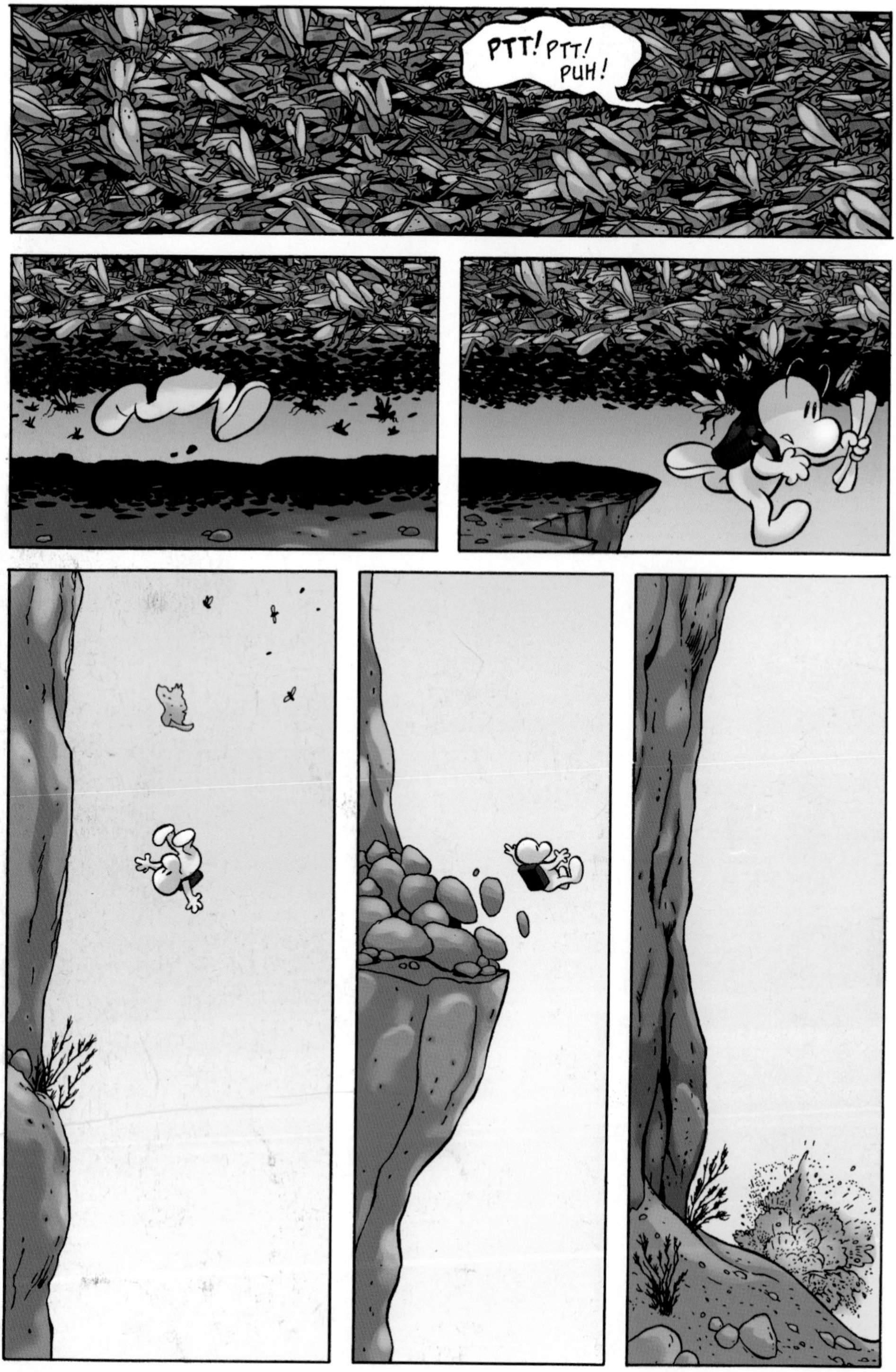
PTT! PTT! PUH!

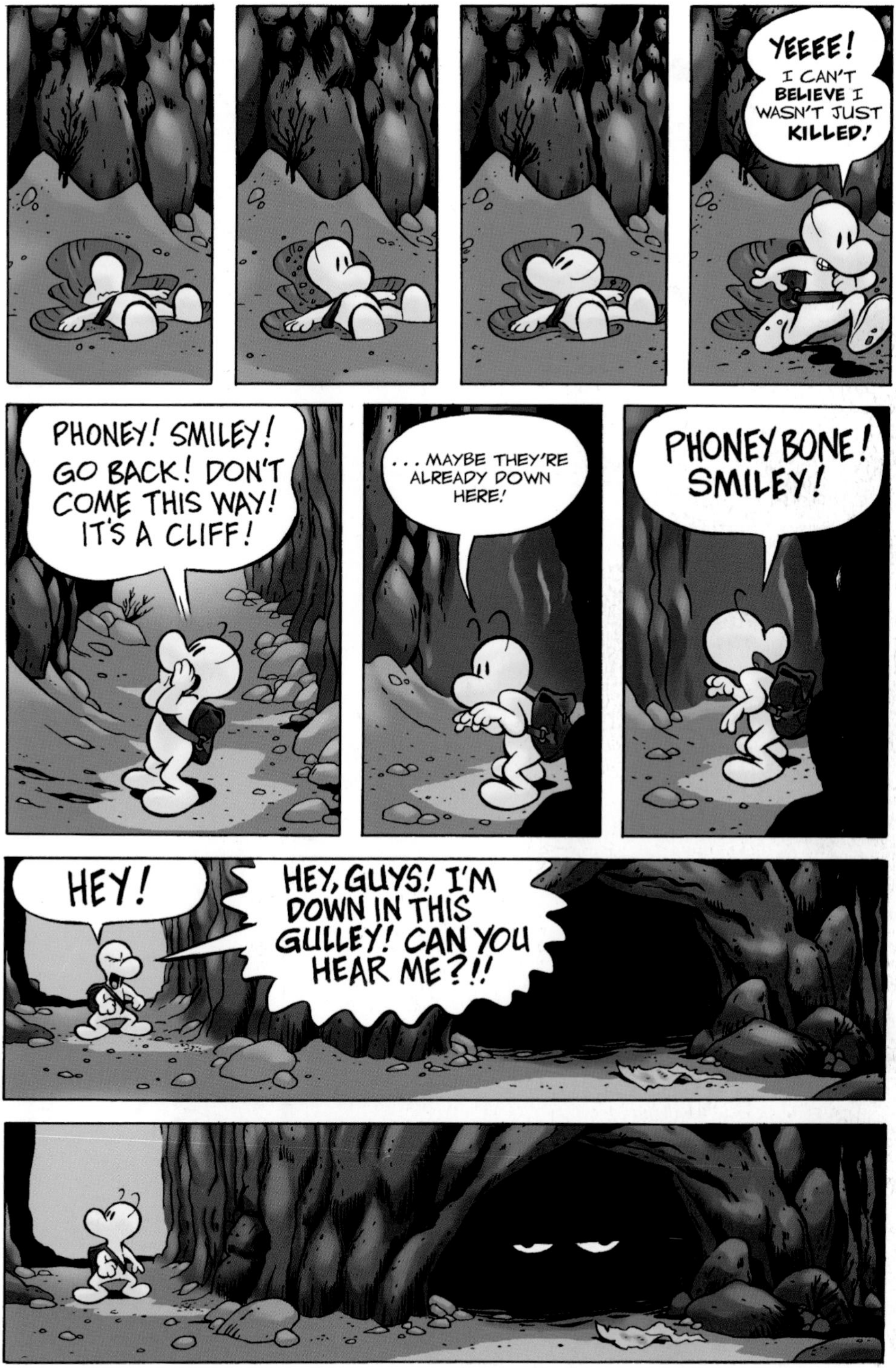
YEEEE! I CAN'T BELIEVE I WASN'T JUST KILLED!
PHONEY! SMILEY! GO BACK! DON'T COME THIS WAY! IT'S A CLIFF!
...MAYBE THEY'RE ALREADY DOWN HERE!
PHONEY BONE! SMILEY!
HEY!
HEY, GUYS! I'M DOWN IN THIS GULLEY! CAN YOU HEAR ME?!!

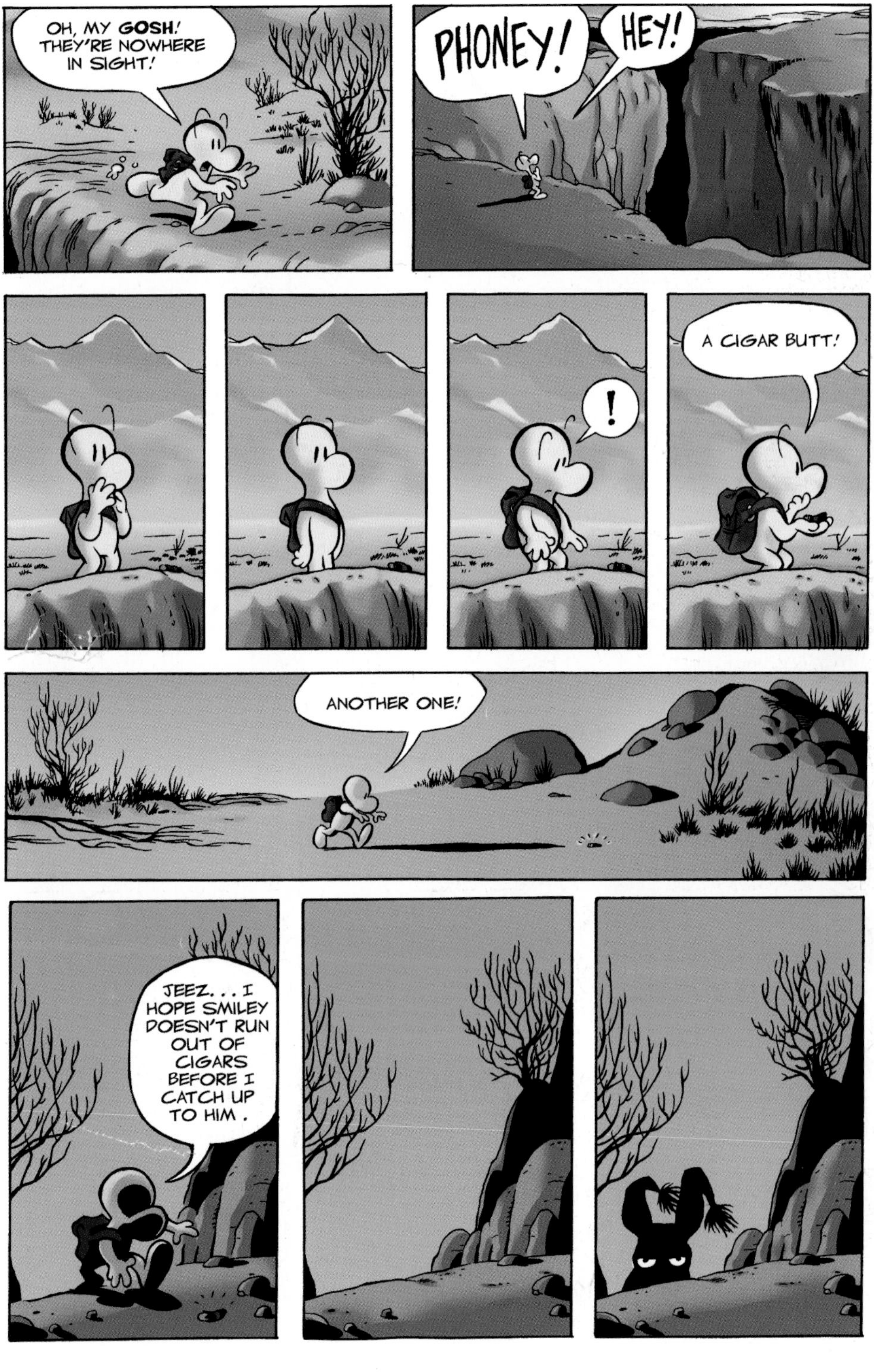
OH, MY GOSH! THEY'RE NOWHERE IN SIGHT!
PHONEY!
HEY!
!
A CIGAR BUTT!
ANOTHER ONE!
JEEZ. . . I HOPE SMILEY DOESN'T RUN OUT OF CIGARS BEFORE I CATCH UP TO HIM.

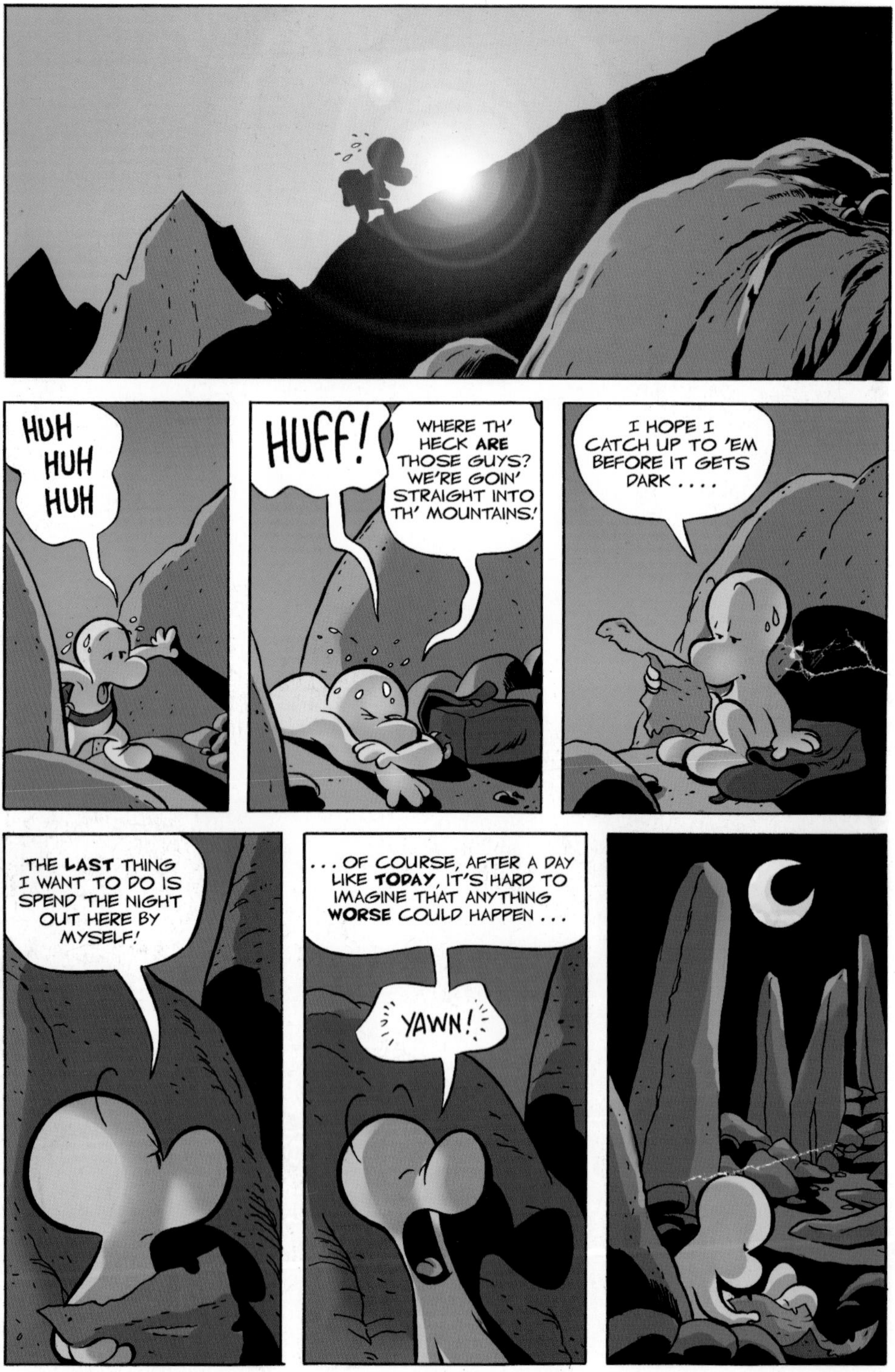
HUH HUH HUH
HUFF!
WHERE TH' HECK ARE THOSE GUYS? WE'RE GOIN' STRAIGHT INTO TH' MOUNTAINS!
I HOPE I CATCH UP TO 'EM BEFORE IT GETS DARK . . . .
THE LAST THING I WANT TO DO IS SPEND THE NIGHT OUT HERE BY MYSELF!
. . . OF COURSE, AFTER A DAY LIKE TODAY, IT'S HARD TO IMAGINE THAT ANYTHING WORSE COULD HAPPEN . . .
YAWN!

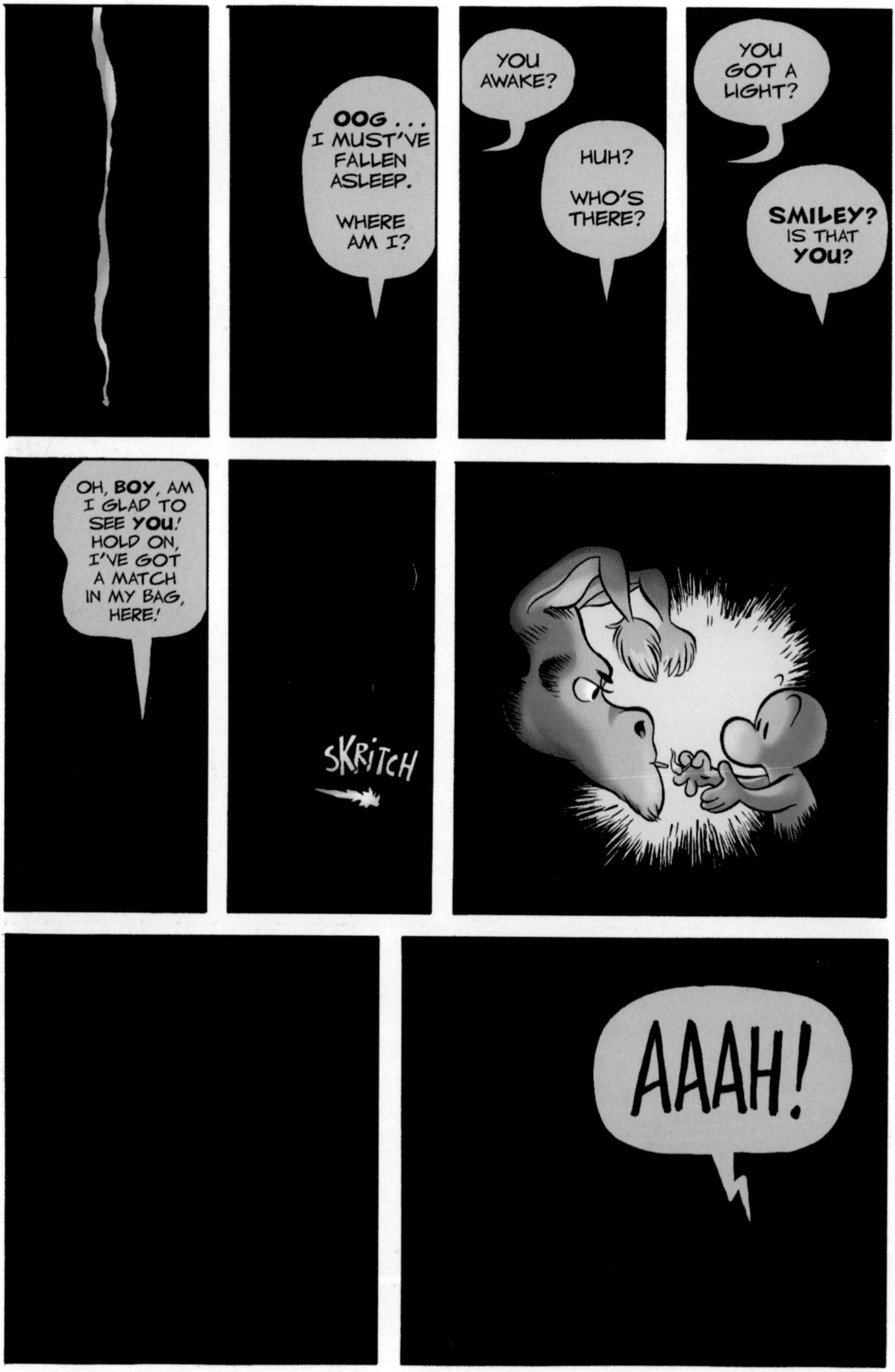
OOG . . . I MUST'VE FALLEN ASLEEP. WHERE AM I?
YOU AWAKE?
HUH? WHO'S THERE?
YOU GOT A LIGHT?
SMILEY? IS THAT YOU?
OH, BOY, AM I GLAD TO SEE YOU! HOLD ON, I'VE GOT A MATCH IN MY BAG, HERE!
SKRITCH
AAAH!

THE MAP

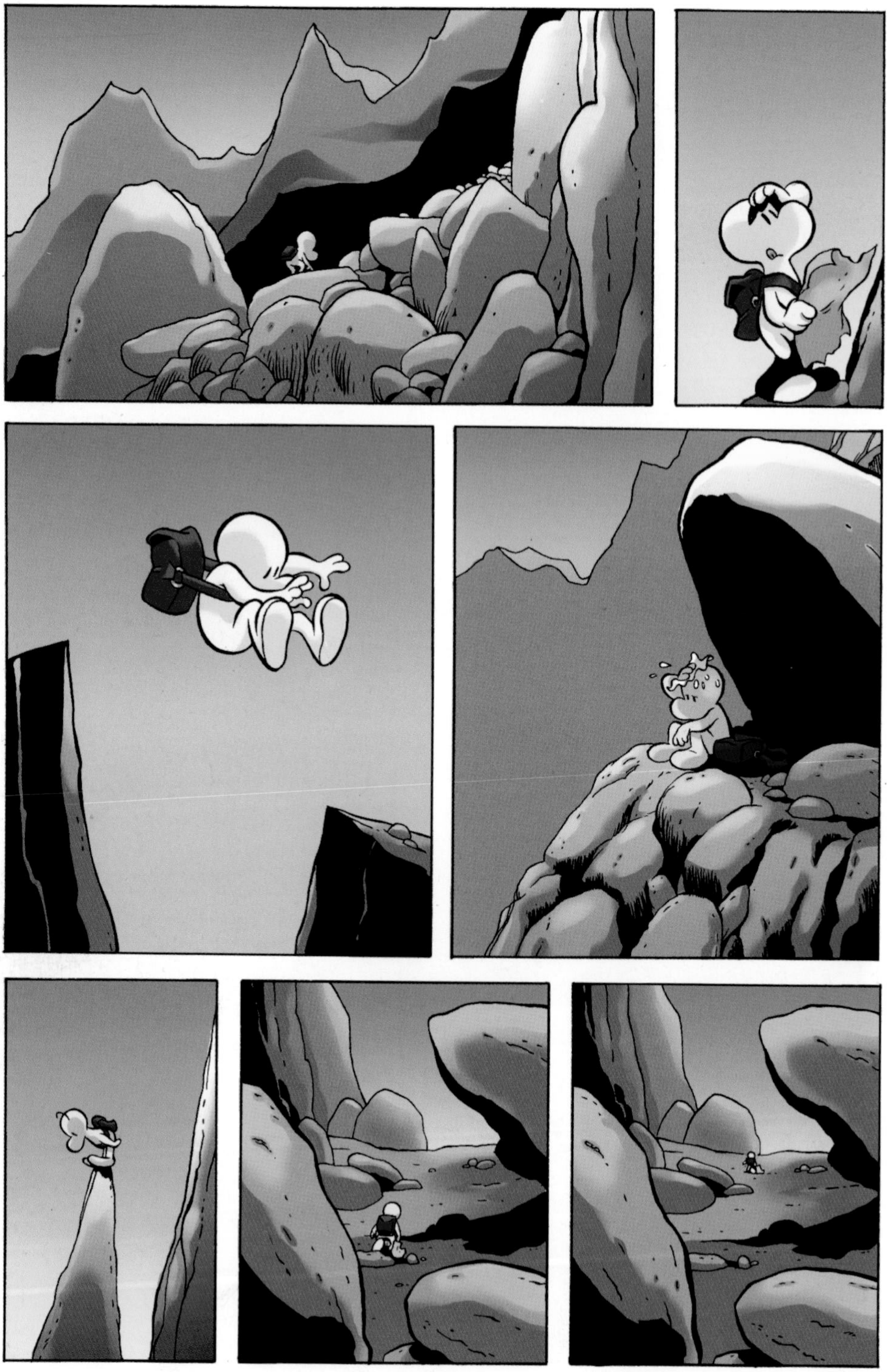

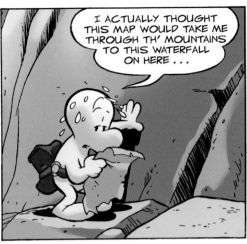

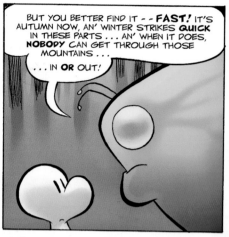

BUT YOU BETTER FIND IT - - **FAST!** IT'S AUTUMN NOW, AN' WINTER STRIKES **QUICK** IN THESE PARTS ... AN' WHEN IT DOES, **NOBODY** CAN GET THROUGH THOSE MOUNTAINS ...

... IN **OR** OUT!

SO I SUGGEST YOU MAKE YOUR VISIT HERE A **SHORT** ONE, OR YOU'LL BE STUCK FOR TH' WINTER. AN' I DON'T THINK YOU WANNA **DO** THAT!

NO. DEFINITELY NOT.

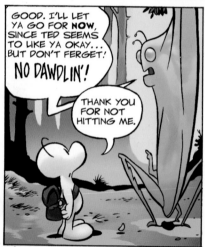

GOOD. I'LL LET YA GO FOR **NOW,** SINCE TED SEEMS TO LIKE YA OKAY... BUT DON'T FERGET! **NO DAWDLIN'!**

THANK YOU FOR NOT HITTING ME.

DON'T WORRY 'BOUT HIM... HE'S ACTUAL A REAL NICE GUY!

WELL... NOW WE GOTTA FIGGER OUT WHAT TA **DO** WITH YA ... SAY! I KNOW! I'LL TAKE YA TO SEE THORN! C'MON! WHAT'S YER **NAME,** MISTER?

FONE BONE. SO WHO'S THIS THORN? HE'S NOT ANOTHER **BIG BUG,** IS HE?

HO, HO! NO! THORN KNOWS JES' ABOUT EVER'THIN' IN TH' **WHOLE WORLD!**

BUT, LISTEN, BONE! BIG BROTHER WAS RIGHT ABOUT WINTER! SHE HITS **FAST!** 'N' IF YOU WANTS TA GIT HOME, YOU GOTTA DO IT BEFORE SHE **SNOWS!**

DON'T WORRY! I'M JUST GONNA FIND MY COUSINS, AN' THEN I'M **OUTTA HERE!**

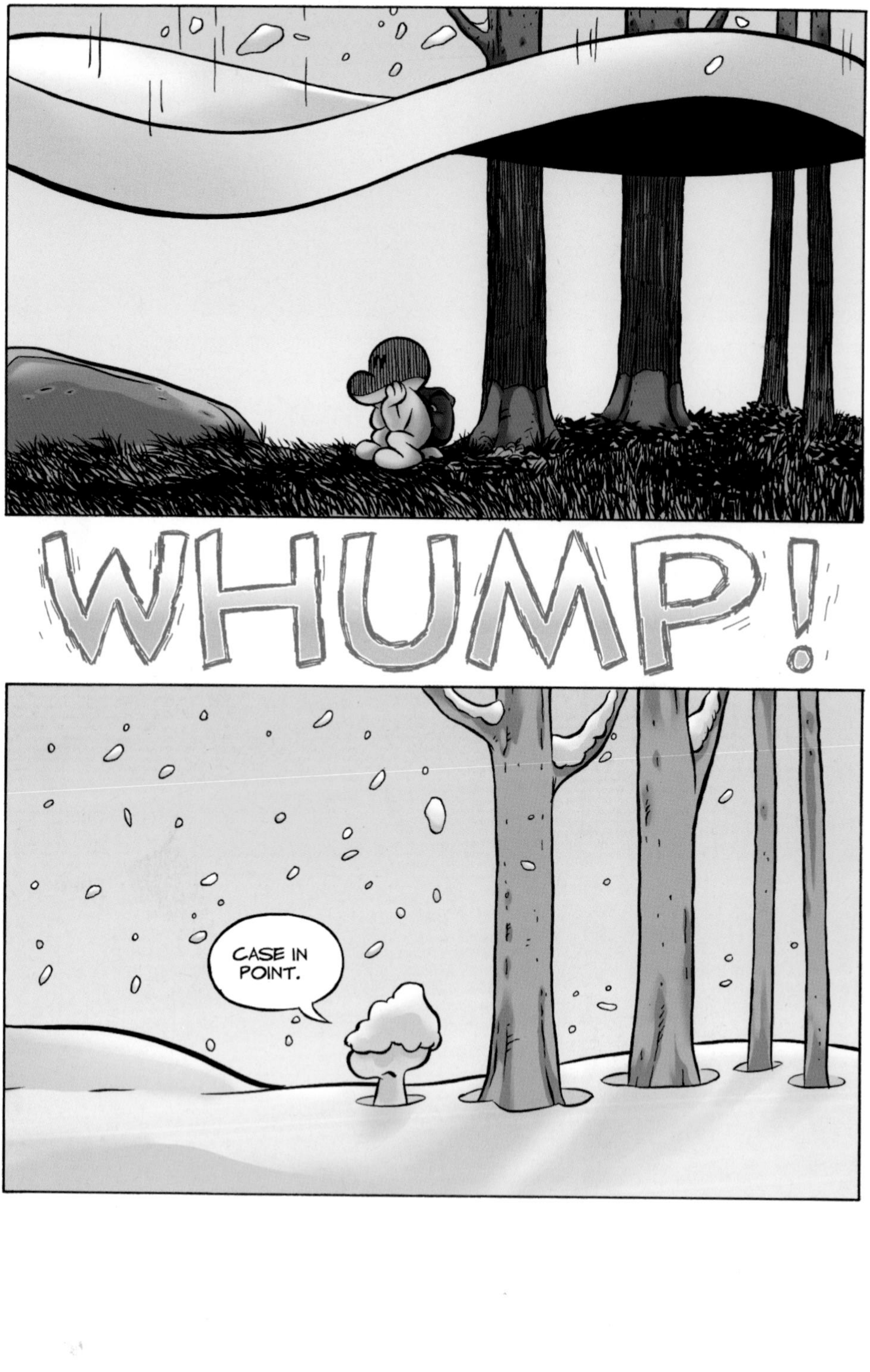
WHUMP!
CASE IN POINT.

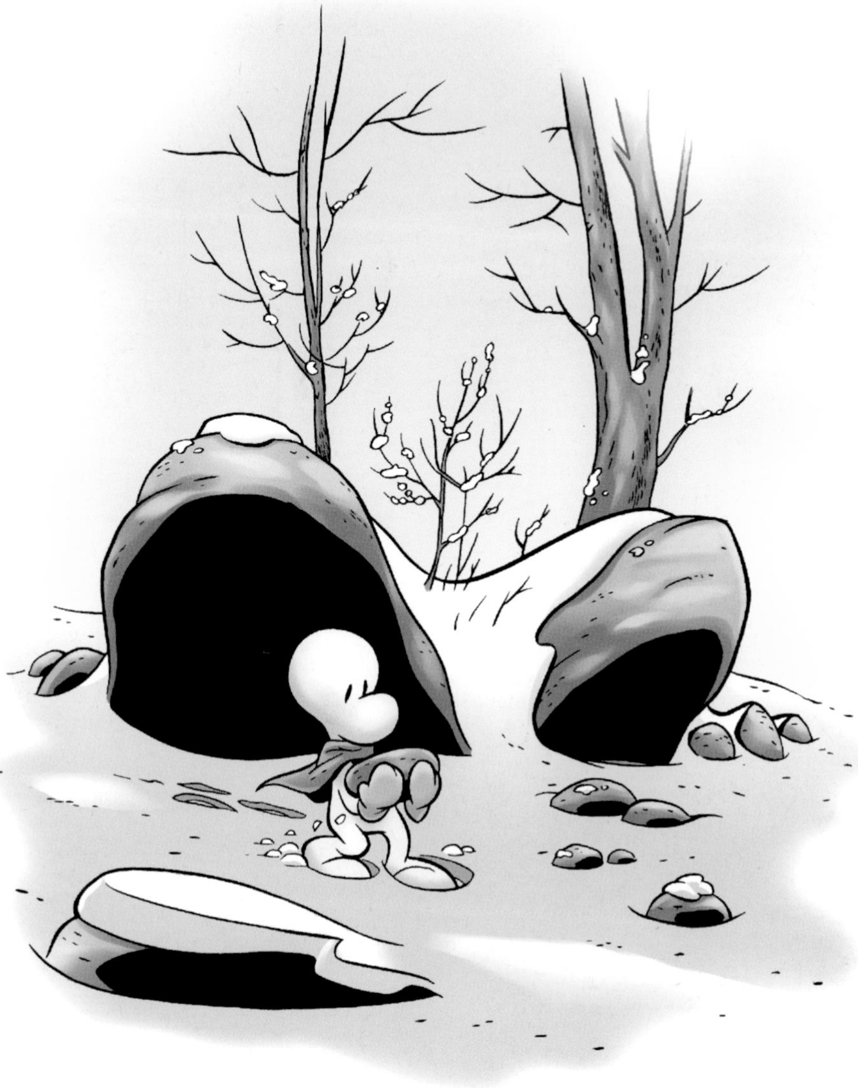

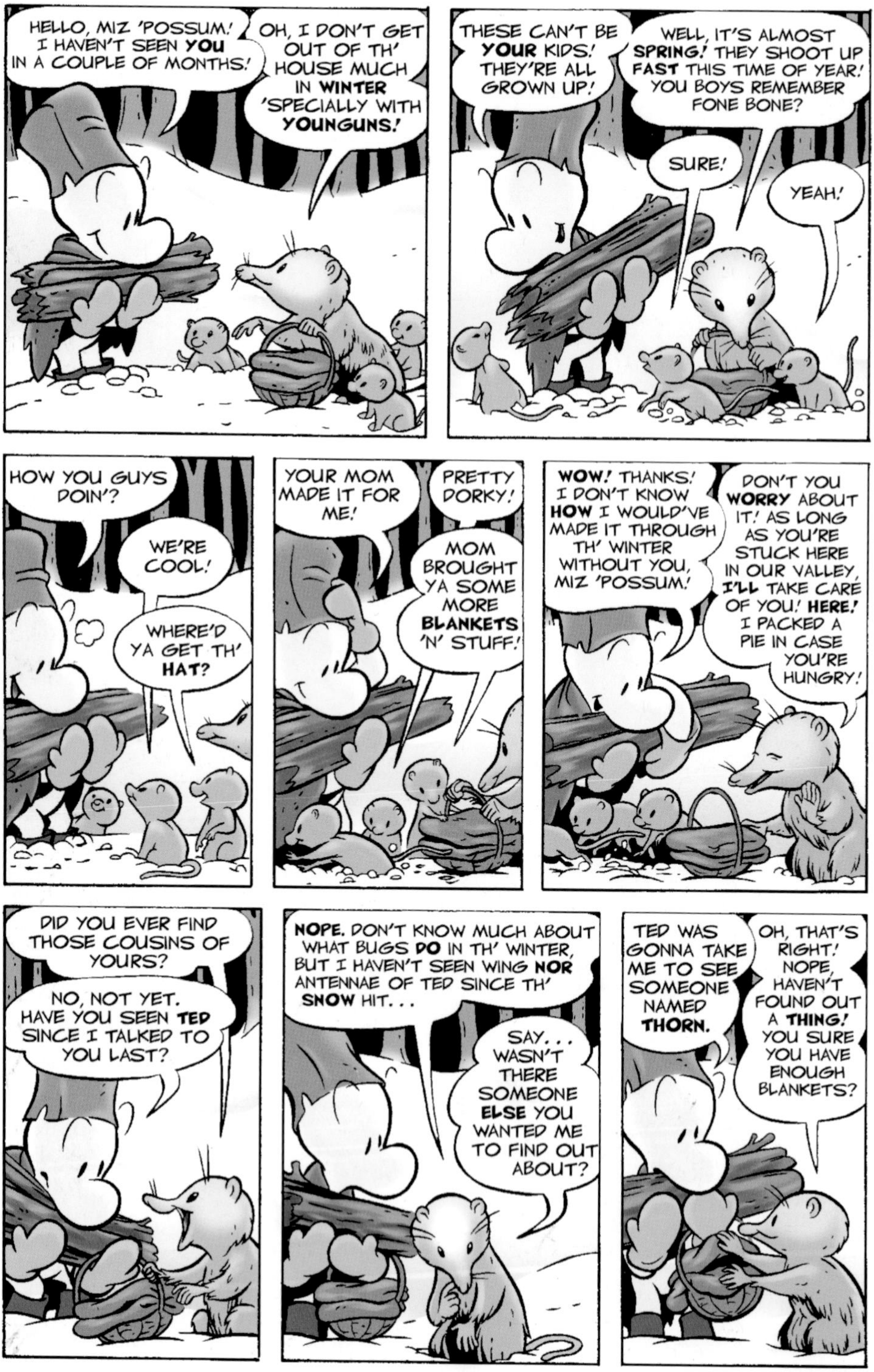
HELLO, MIZ 'POSSUM! I HAVEN'T SEEN YOU IN A COUPLE OF MONTHS!
OH, I DON'T GET OUT OF TH' HOUSE MUCH IN WINTER 'SPECIALLY WITH YOUNGUNS!
THESE CAN'T BE YOUR KIDS! THEY'RE ALL GROWN UP!
WELL, IT'S ALMOST SPRING! THEY SHOOT UP FAST THIS TIME OF YEAR! YOU BOYS REMEMBER FONE BONE?
SURE!
YEAH!
HOW YOU GUYS DOIN'?
WE'RE COOL!
WHERE'D YA GET TH' HAT?
YOUR MOM MADE IT FOR ME!
PRETTY DORKY!
MOM BROUGHT YA SOME MORE BLANKETS 'N' STUFF!
WOW! THANKS! I DON'T KNOW HOW I WOULD'VE MADE IT THROUGH TH' WINTER WITHOUT YOU, MIZ 'POSSUM!
DON'T YOU WORRY ABOUT IT! AS LONG AS YOU'RE STUCK HERE IN OUR VALLEY, I'LL TAKE CARE OF YOU! HERE! I PACKED A PIE IN CASE YOU'RE HUNGRY!
DID YOU EVER FIND THOSE COUSINS OF YOURS?
NO, NOT YET. HAVE YOU SEEN TED SINCE I TALKED TO YOU LAST?
NOPE. DON'T KNOW MUCH ABOUT WHAT BUGS DO IN TH' WINTER, BUT I HAVEN'T SEEN WING NOR ANTENNAE OF TED SINCE TH' SNOW HIT...
SAY... WASN'T THERE SOMEONE ELSE YOU WANTED ME TO FIND OUT ABOUT?
TED WAS GONNA TAKE ME TO SEE SOMEONE NAMED THORN.
OH, THAT'S RIGHT! NOPE, HAVEN'T FOUND OUT A THING! YOU SURE YOU HAVE ENOUGH BLANKETS?

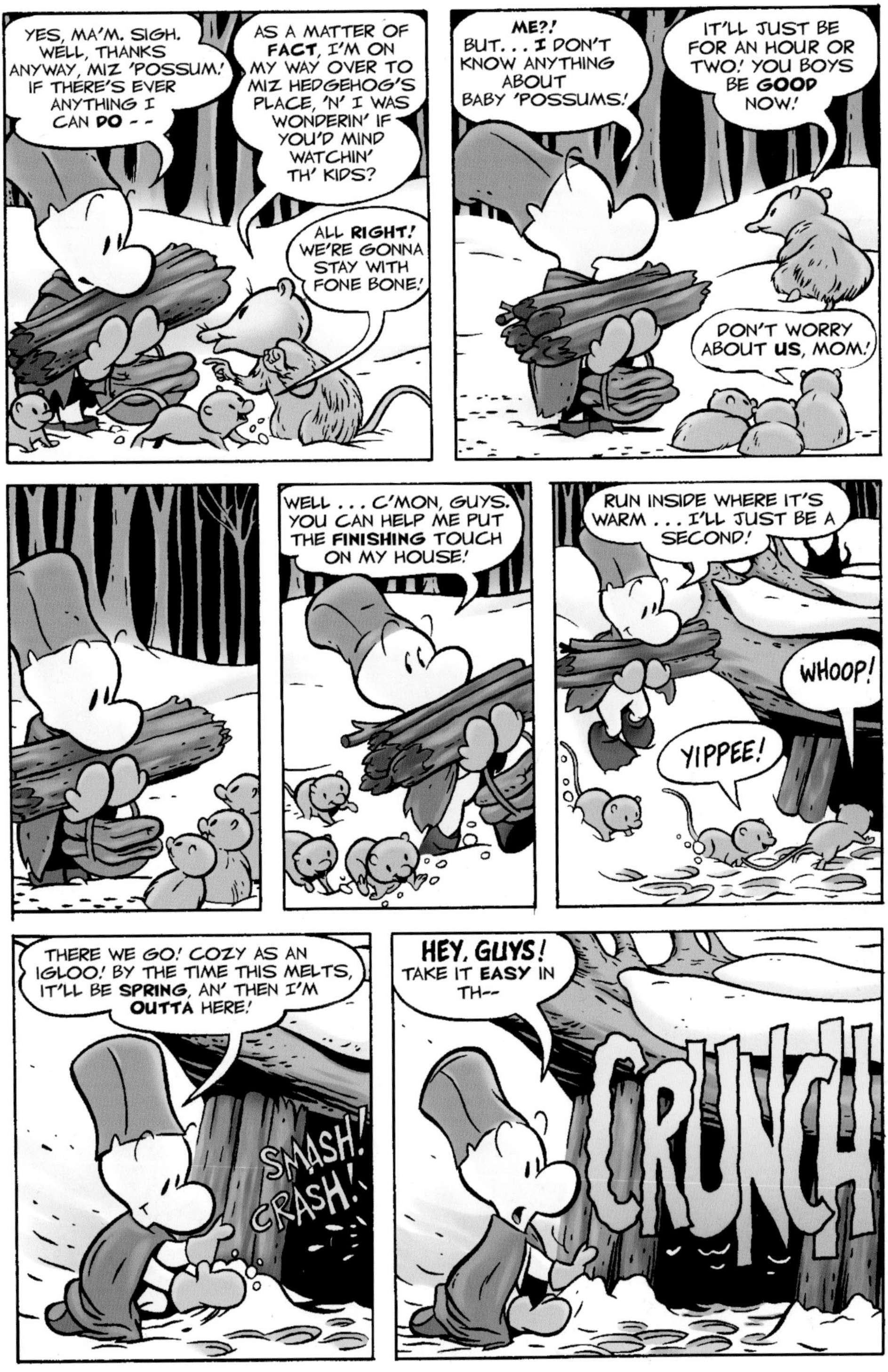
YES, MA'M. SIGH. WELL, THANKS ANYWAY, MIZ 'POSSUM! IF THERE'S EVER ANYTHING I CAN DO - -
AS A MATTER OF FACT, I'M ON MY WAY OVER TO MIZ HEDGEHOG'S PLACE, 'N' I WAS WONDERIN' IF YOU'D MIND WATCHIN' TH' KIDS?
ALL RIGHT! WE'RE GONNA STAY WITH FONE BONE!
ME?! BUT. . . I DON'T KNOW ANYTHING ABOUT BABY 'POSSUMS!
IT'LL JUST BE FOR AN HOUR OR TWO! YOU BOYS BE GOOD NOW!
DON'T WORRY ABOUT US, MOM!
WELL . . . C'MON, GUYS. YOU CAN HELP ME PUT THE FINISHING TOUCH ON MY HOUSE!
RUN INSIDE WHERE IT'S WARM . . . I'LL JUST BE A SECOND!
WHOOP!
YIPPEE!
THERE WE GO! COZY AS AN IGLOO! BY THE TIME THIS MELTS, IT'LL BE SPRING, AN' THEN I'M OUTTA HERE!
SMASH!
CRASH!
HEY, GUYS! TAKE IT EASY IN TH--
CRUNCH

WHAT TH' HECK WAS THAT?

HOLY COW!

WHAT ARE YOU TRYING TO **DO**?!! **KILL** EACH OTHER? C'MON, LET'S SIT BY THE FIREPLACE, AN' I'LL TELL YOU A STORY!

AW! WE WERE HAVIN' **FUN!**

WE DON'T **WANNA** HEAR A STORY!

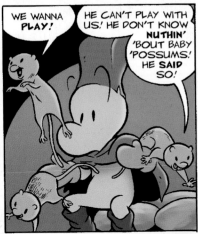

WE WANNA **PLAY!**

HE CAN'T PLAY WITH US! HE DON'T KNOW **NUTHIN'** 'BOUT BABY 'POSSUMS! HE **SAID** SO!

PLAY WITH US, MR. BONE!

YEAH! C'MON!

WHAT DO YOU WANNA PLAY?

WHAT 'POSSUMS PLAY **BEST** IS PLAY "DEAD"!

LOOK OUT! IT'S A GIANT 'POSSUM-EATING BEAR!!

THOSE RAT CREATURES WOULD HAVE TO BE PRETTY STUPID TO FOLLOW ME ON TO THIS FRAIL, LITTLE BRANCH!

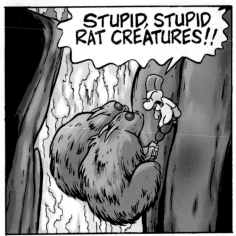

STUPID, STUPID RAT CREATURES!!

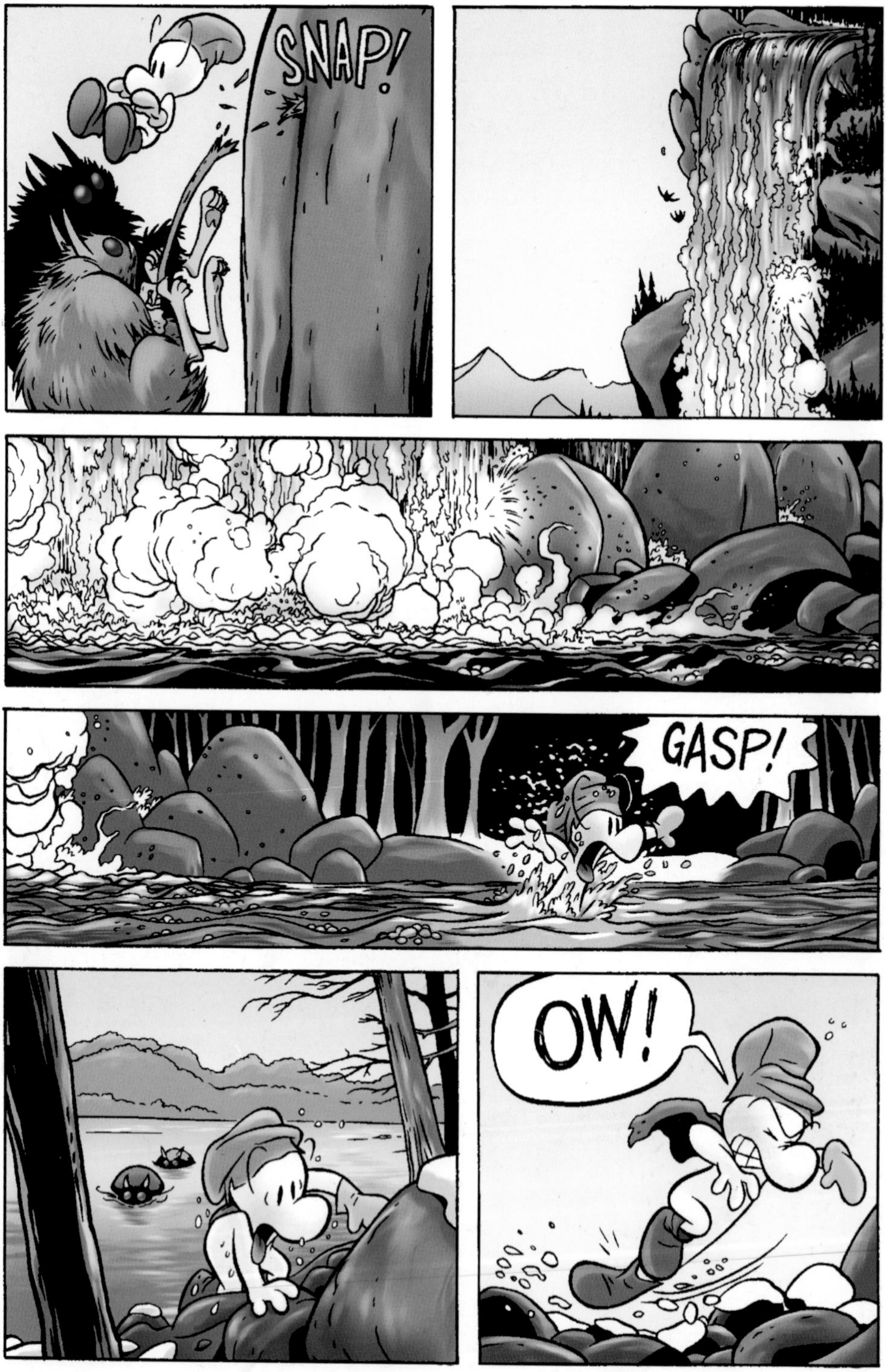
SNAP!
GASP!
OW!

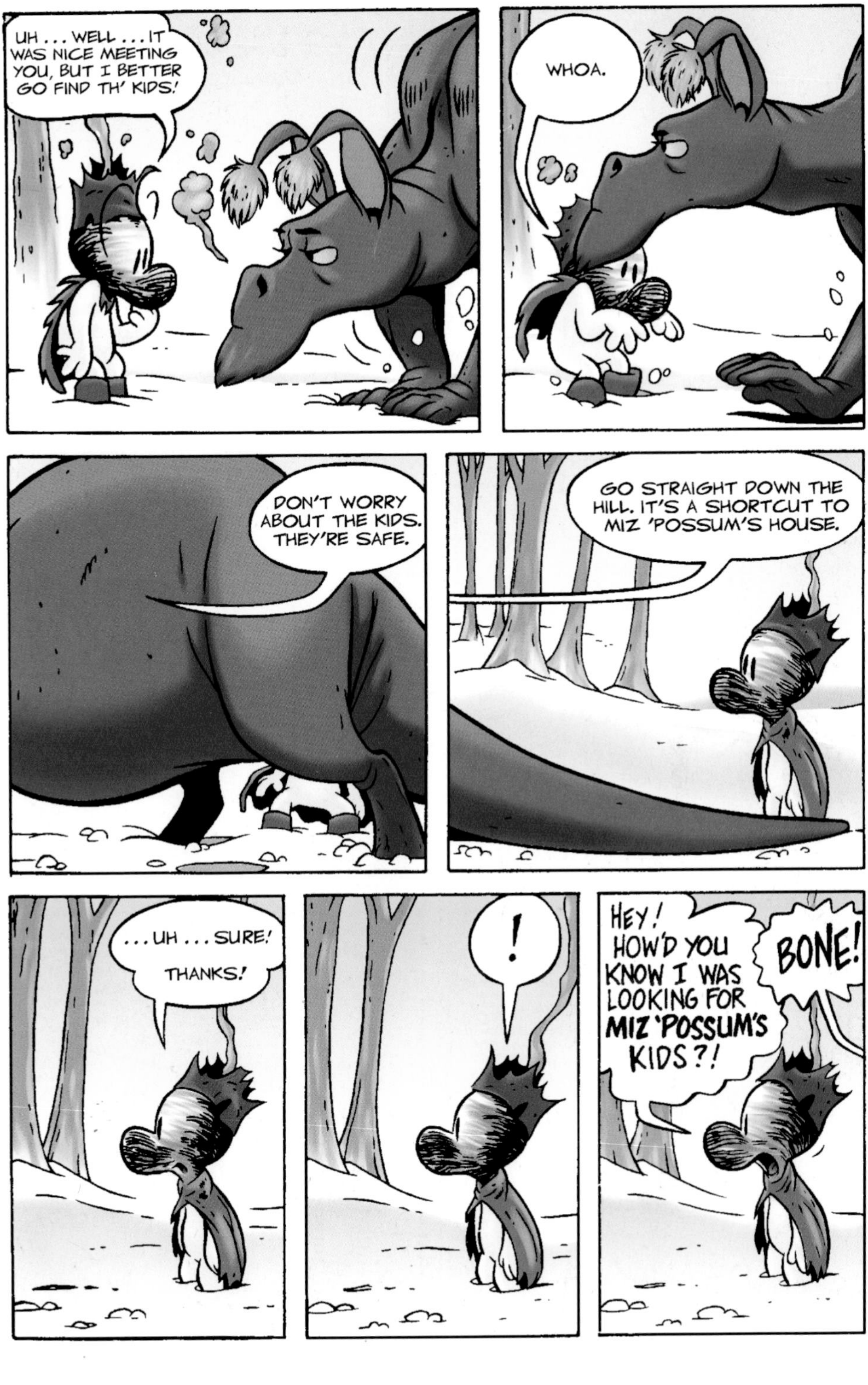
UH . . . WELL . . . IT WAS NICE MEETING YOU, BUT I BETTER GO FIND TH' KIDS!
WHOA.
DON'T WORRY ABOUT THE KIDS. THEY'RE SAFE.
GO STRAIGHT DOWN THE HILL. IT'S A SHORTCUT TO MIZ 'POSSUM'S HOUSE.
. . . UH . . . SURE!
THANKS!
!
HEY! HOW'D YOU KNOW I WAS LOOKING FOR MIZ 'POSSUM'S KIDS?!
BONE!

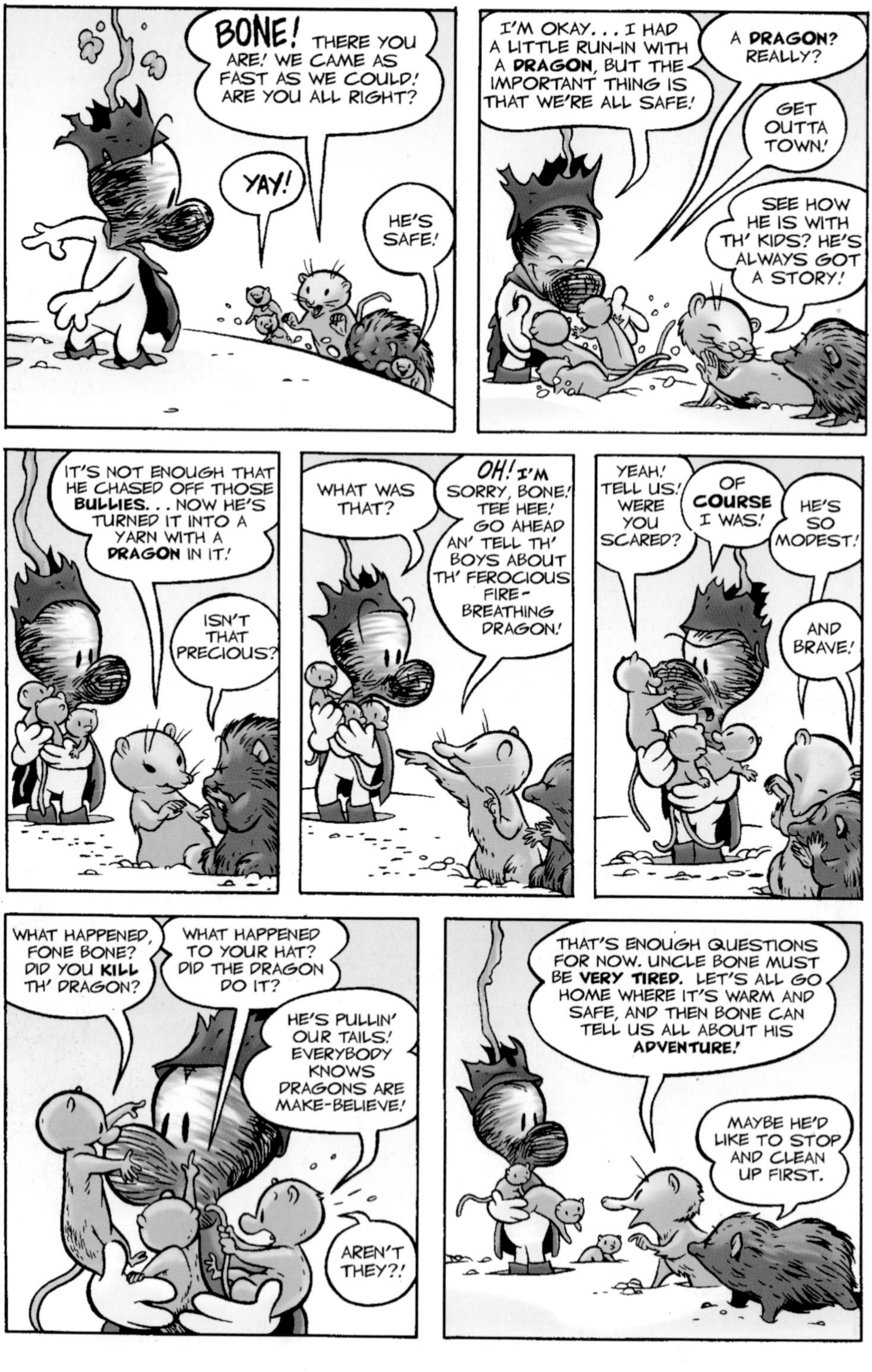
BONE! THERE YOU ARE! WE CAME AS FAST AS WE COULD! ARE YOU ALL RIGHT?
YAY!
HE'S SAFE!
I'M OKAY. . . I HAD A LITTLE RUN-IN WITH A DRAGON, BUT THE IMPORTANT THING IS THAT WE'RE ALL SAFE!
A DRAGON? REALLY?
GET OUTTA TOWN!
SEE HOW HE IS WITH TH' KIDS? HE'S ALWAYS GOT A STORY!
IT'S NOT ENOUGH THAT HE CHASED OFF THOSE BULLIES. . . NOW HE'S TURNED IT INTO A YARN WITH A DRAGON IN IT!
ISN'T THAT PRECIOUS?
WHAT WAS THAT?
OH! I'M SORRY, BONE! TEE HEE! GO AHEAD AN' TELL TH' BOYS ABOUT TH' FEROCIOUS FIRE-BREATHING DRAGON!
YEAH! TELL US! WERE YOU SCARED?
OF COURSE I WAS!
HE'S SO MODEST!
AND BRAVE!
WHAT HAPPENED, FONE BONE? DID YOU KILL TH' DRAGON?
WHAT HAPPENED TO YOUR HAT? DID THE DRAGON DO IT?
HE'S PULLIN' OUR TAILS! EVERYBODY KNOWS DRAGONS ARE MAKE-BELIEVE!
AREN'T THEY?!
THAT'S ENOUGH QUESTIONS FOR NOW. UNCLE BONE MUST BE VERY TIRED. LET'S ALL GO HOME WHERE IT'S WARM AND SAFE, AND THEN BONE CAN TELL US ALL ABOUT HIS ADVENTURE!
MAYBE HE'D LIKE TO STOP AND CLEAN UP FIRST.

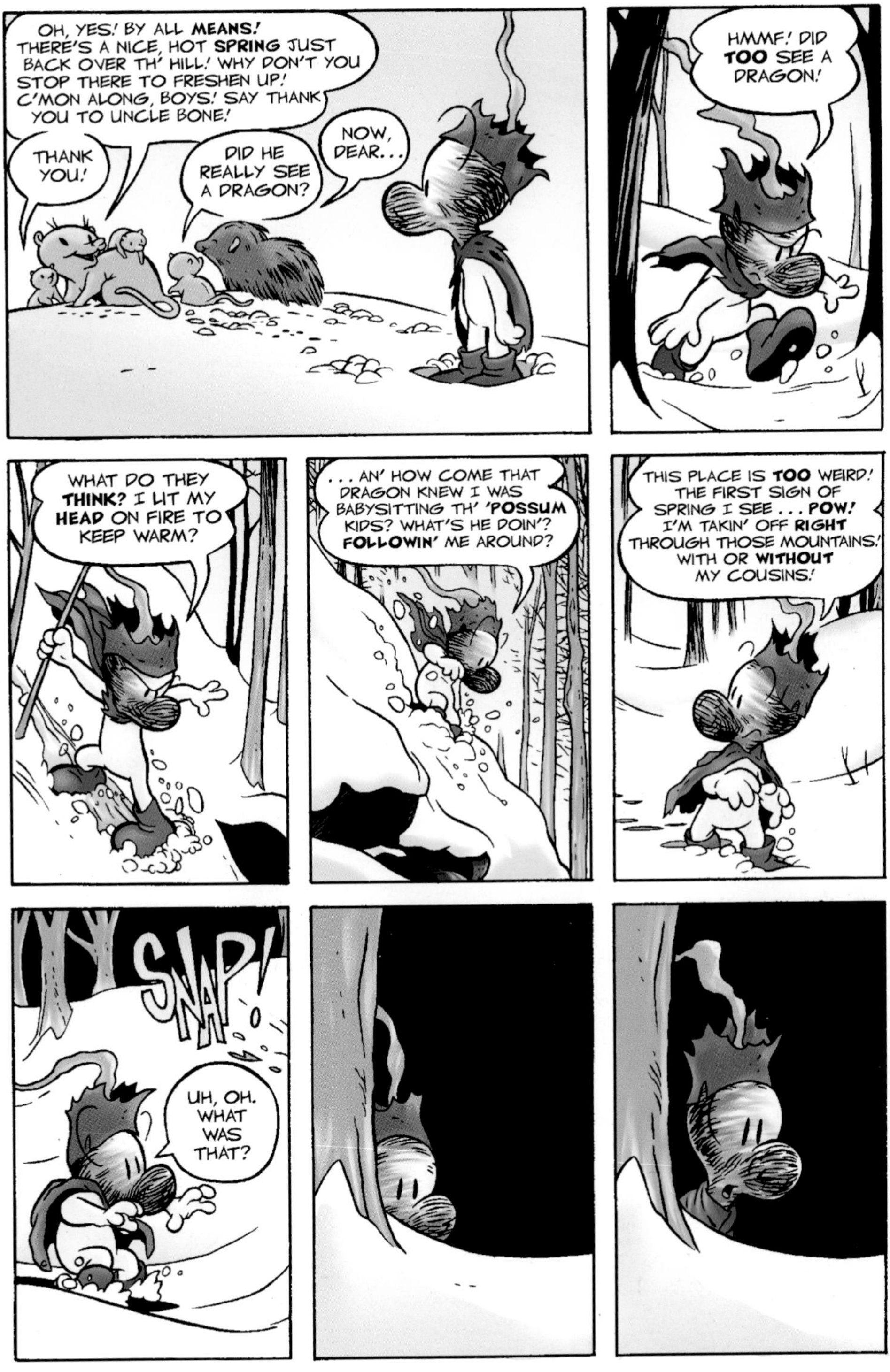
OH, YES! BY ALL MEANS! THERE'S A NICE, HOT SPRING JUST BACK OVER TH' HILL! WHY DON'T YOU STOP THERE TO FRESHEN UP! C'MON ALONG, BOYS! SAY THANK YOU TO UNCLE BONE!
THANK YOU!
DID HE REALLY SEE A DRAGON?
NOW, DEAR...
HMMF! DID TOO SEE A DRAGON!
WHAT DO THEY THINK? I LIT MY HEAD ON FIRE TO KEEP WARM?
...AN' HOW COME THAT DRAGON KNEW I WAS BABYSITTING TH' 'POSSUM KIDS? WHAT'S HE DOIN'? FOLLOWIN' ME AROUND?
THIS PLACE IS TOO WEIRD! THE FIRST SIGN OF SPRING I SEE... POW! I'M TAKIN' OFF RIGHT THROUGH THOSE MOUNTAINS! WITH OR WITHOUT MY COUSINS!
SNAP!
UH, OH. WHAT WAS THAT?

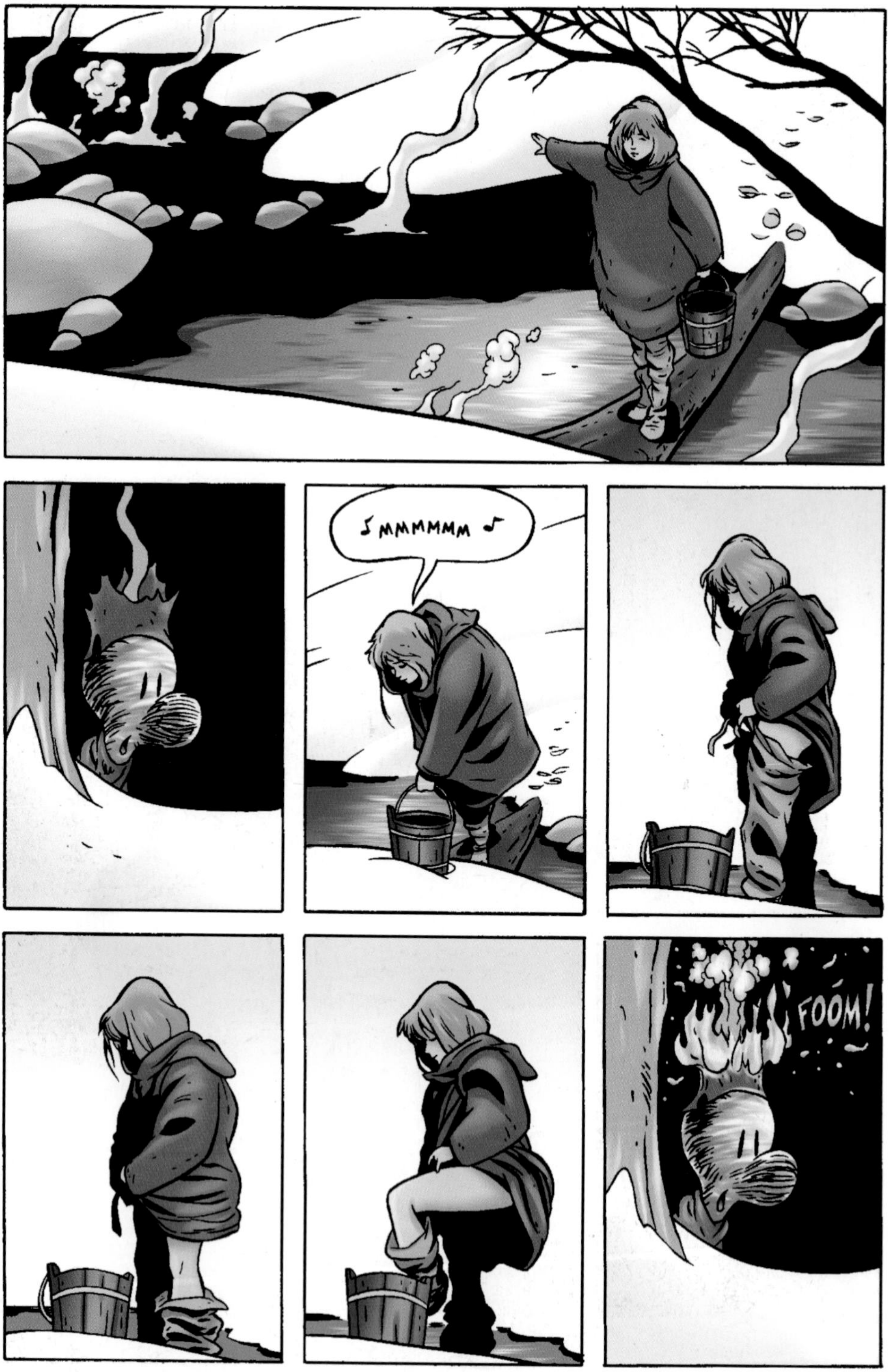
♩MMMMMM♪
FOOM!

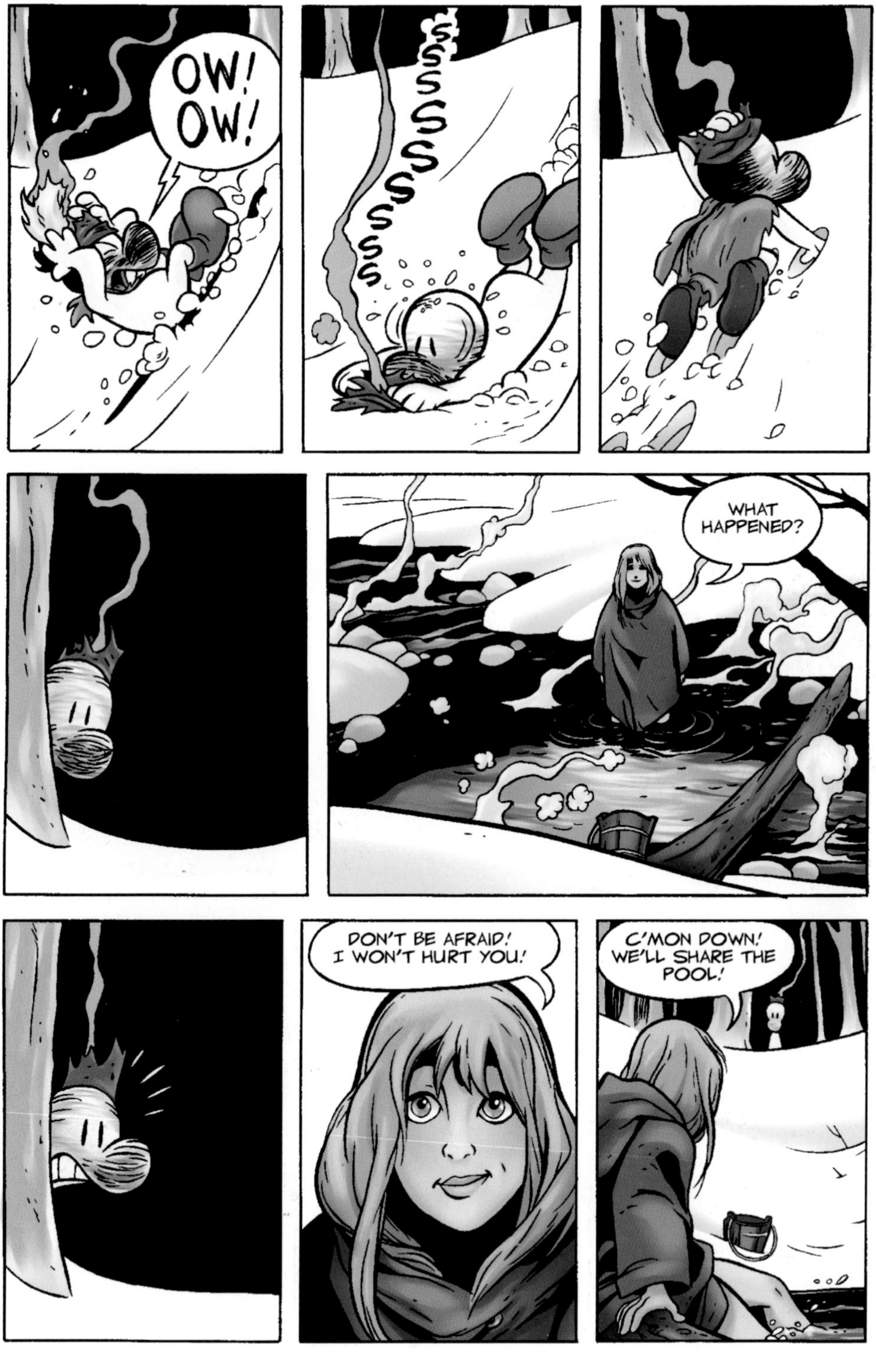
OW! OW!
SSSSSSSSSS
WHAT HAPPENED?
DON'T BE AFRAID! I WON'T HURT YOU!
C'MON DOWN! WE'LL SHARE THE POOL!

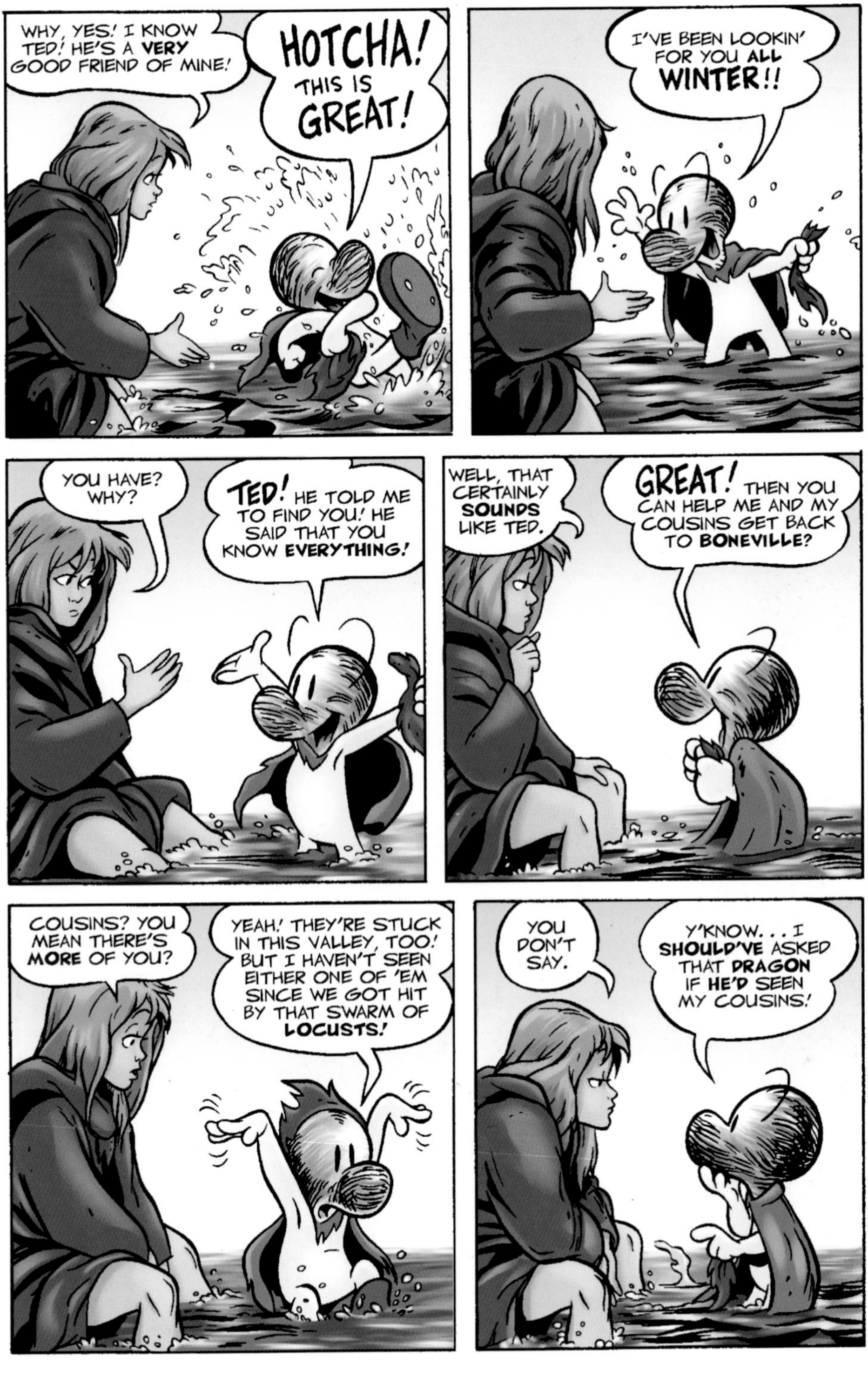
WHY, YES! I KNOW TED! HE'S A VERY GOOD FRIEND OF MINE!
HOTCHA! THIS IS GREAT!
I'VE BEEN LOOKIN' FOR YOU ALL WINTER!!
YOU HAVE? WHY?
TED! HE TOLD ME TO FIND YOU! HE SAID THAT YOU KNOW EVERYTHING!
WELL, THAT CERTAINLY SOUNDS LIKE TED.
GREAT! THEN YOU CAN HELP ME AND MY COUSINS GET BACK TO BONEVILLE?
COUSINS? YOU MEAN THERE'S MORE OF YOU?
YEAH! THEY'RE STUCK IN THIS VALLEY, TOO! BUT I HAVEN'T SEEN EITHER ONE OF 'EM SINCE WE GOT HIT BY THAT SWARM OF LOCUSTS!
YOU DON'T SAY.
Y'KNOW. . . I SHOULD'VE ASKED THAT DRAGON IF HE'D SEEN MY COUSINS!

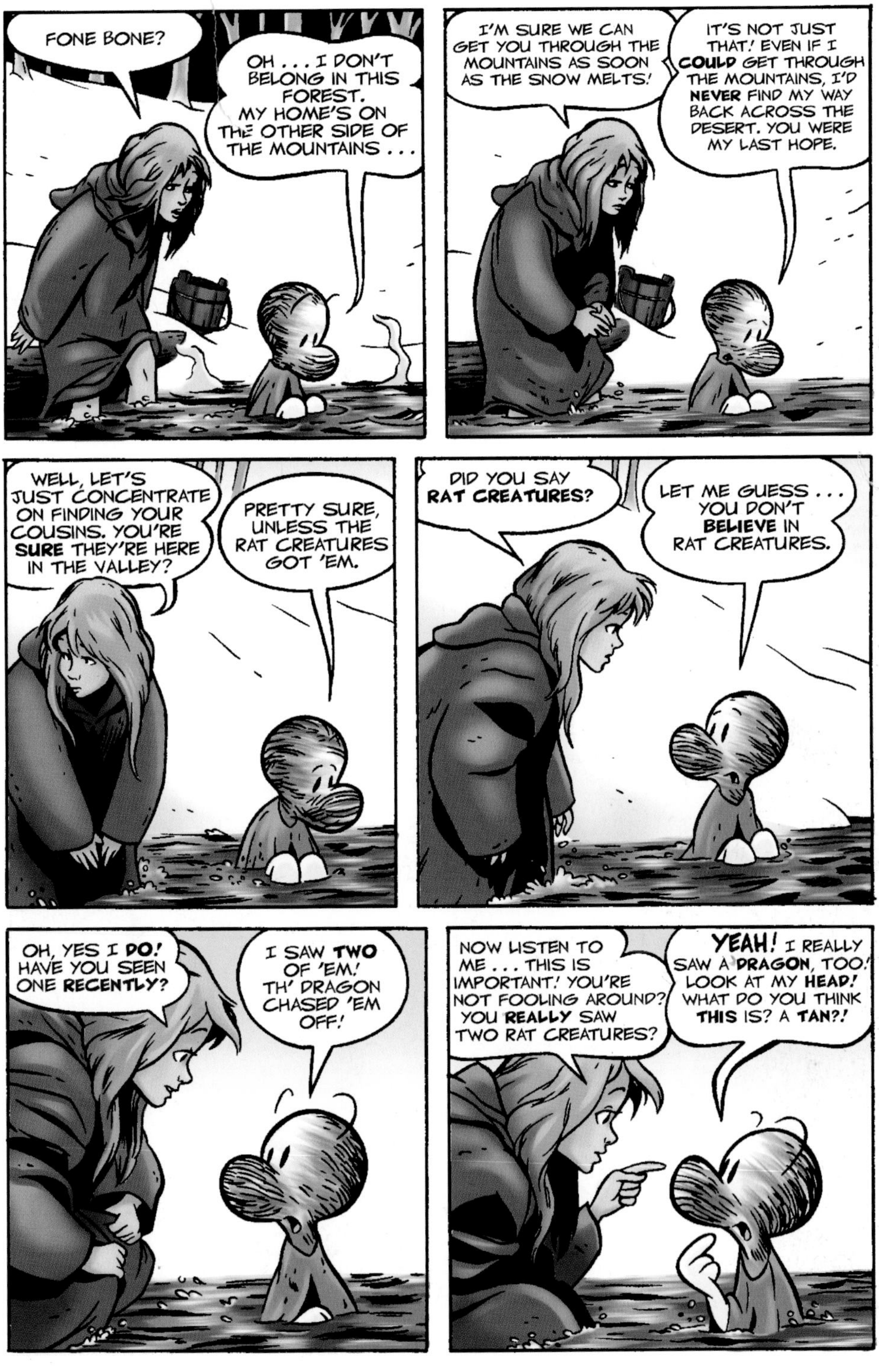
FONE BONE?
OH . . . I DON'T BELONG IN THIS FOREST. MY HOME'S ON THE OTHER SIDE OF THE MOUNTAINS . . .
I'M SURE WE CAN GET YOU THROUGH THE MOUNTAINS AS SOON AS THE SNOW MELTS!
IT'S NOT JUST THAT! EVEN IF I **COULD** GET THROUGH THE MOUNTAINS, I'D **NEVER** FIND MY WAY BACK ACROSS THE DESERT. YOU WERE MY LAST HOPE.
WELL, LET'S JUST CONCENTRATE ON FINDING YOUR COUSINS. YOU'RE **SURE** THEY'RE HERE IN THE VALLEY?
PRETTY SURE, UNLESS THE RAT CREATURES GOT 'EM.
DID YOU SAY **RAT CREATURES?**
LET ME GUESS . . . YOU DON'T **BELIEVE** IN RAT CREATURES.
OH, YES I **DO**! HAVE YOU SEEN ONE **RECENTLY**?
I SAW **TWO** OF 'EM! TH' DRAGON CHASED 'EM OFF!
NOW LISTEN TO ME . . . THIS IS IMPORTANT! YOU'RE NOT FOOLING AROUND? YOU **REALLY** SAW TWO RAT CREATURES?
YEAH! I REALLY SAW A **DRAGON**, TOO! LOOK AT MY **HEAD!** WHAT DO YOU THINK **THIS** IS? A **TAN?!**

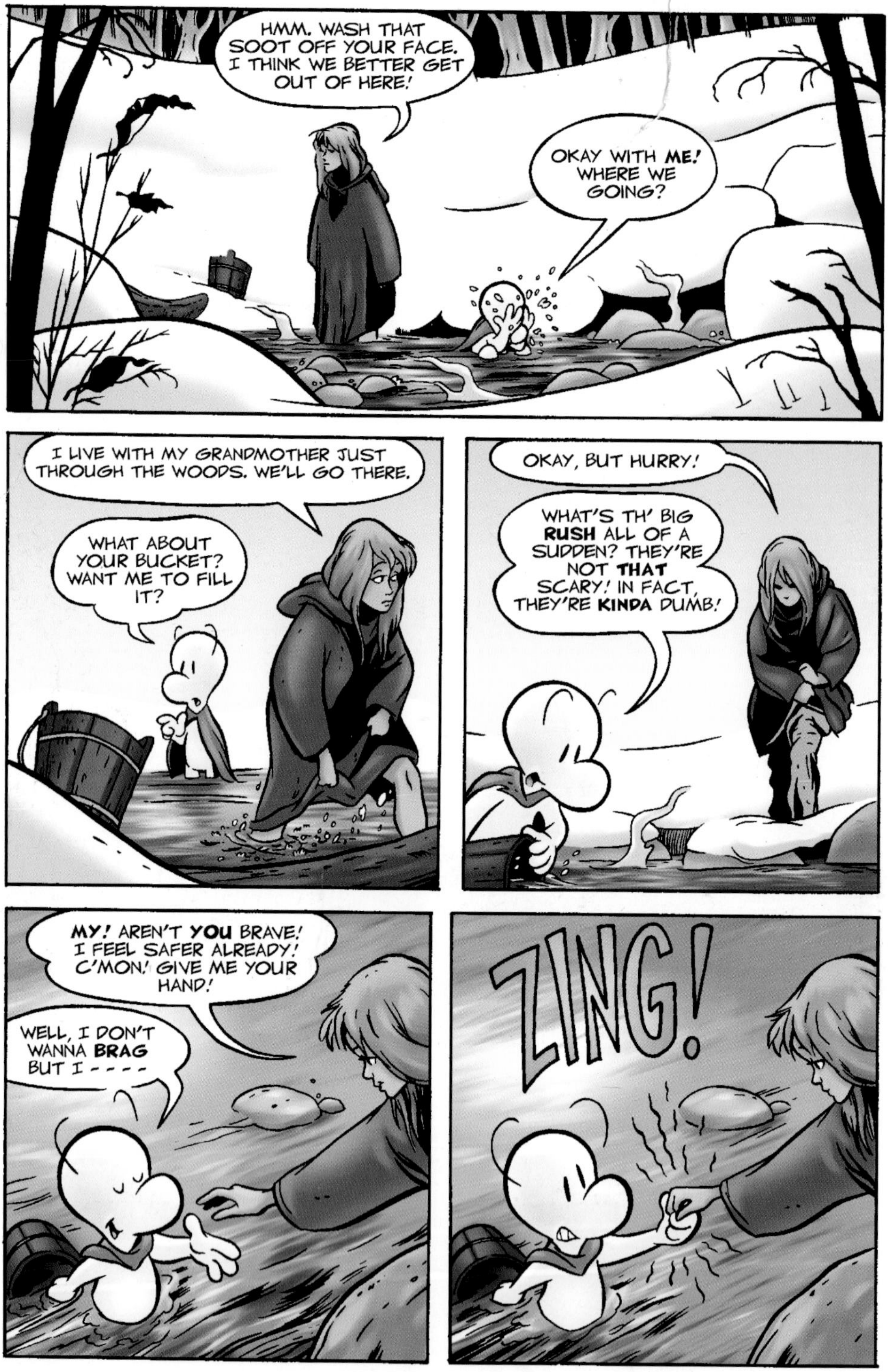
HMM. WASH THAT SOOT OFF YOUR FACE. I THINK WE BETTER GET OUT OF HERE!
OKAY WITH ME! WHERE WE GOING?
I LIVE WITH MY GRANDMOTHER JUST THROUGH THE WOODS. WE'LL GO THERE.
WHAT ABOUT YOUR BUCKET? WANT ME TO FILL IT?
OKAY, BUT HURRY!
WHAT'S TH' BIG RUSH ALL OF A SUDDEN? THEY'RE NOT THAT SCARY! IN FACT, THEY'RE KINDA DUMB!
MY! AREN'T YOU BRAVE! I FEEL SAFER ALREADY! C'MON! GIVE ME YOUR HAND!
WELL, I DON'T WANNA BRAG BUT I - - - -
ZING!

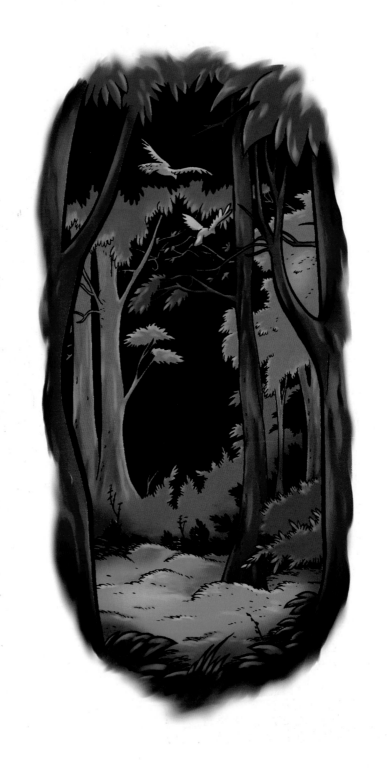

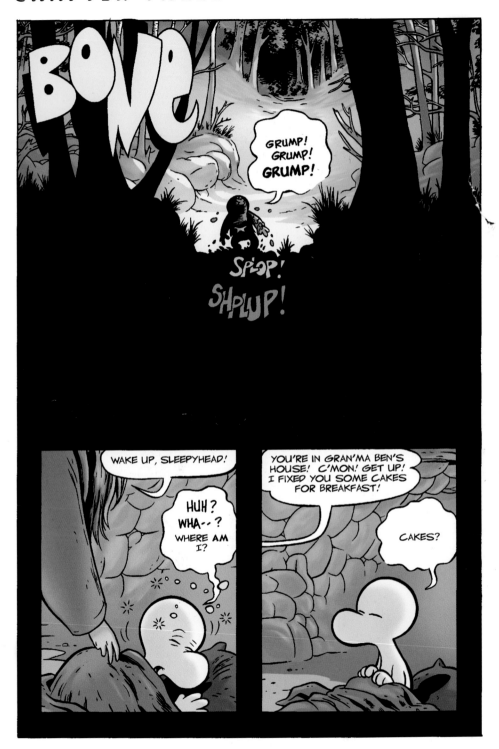

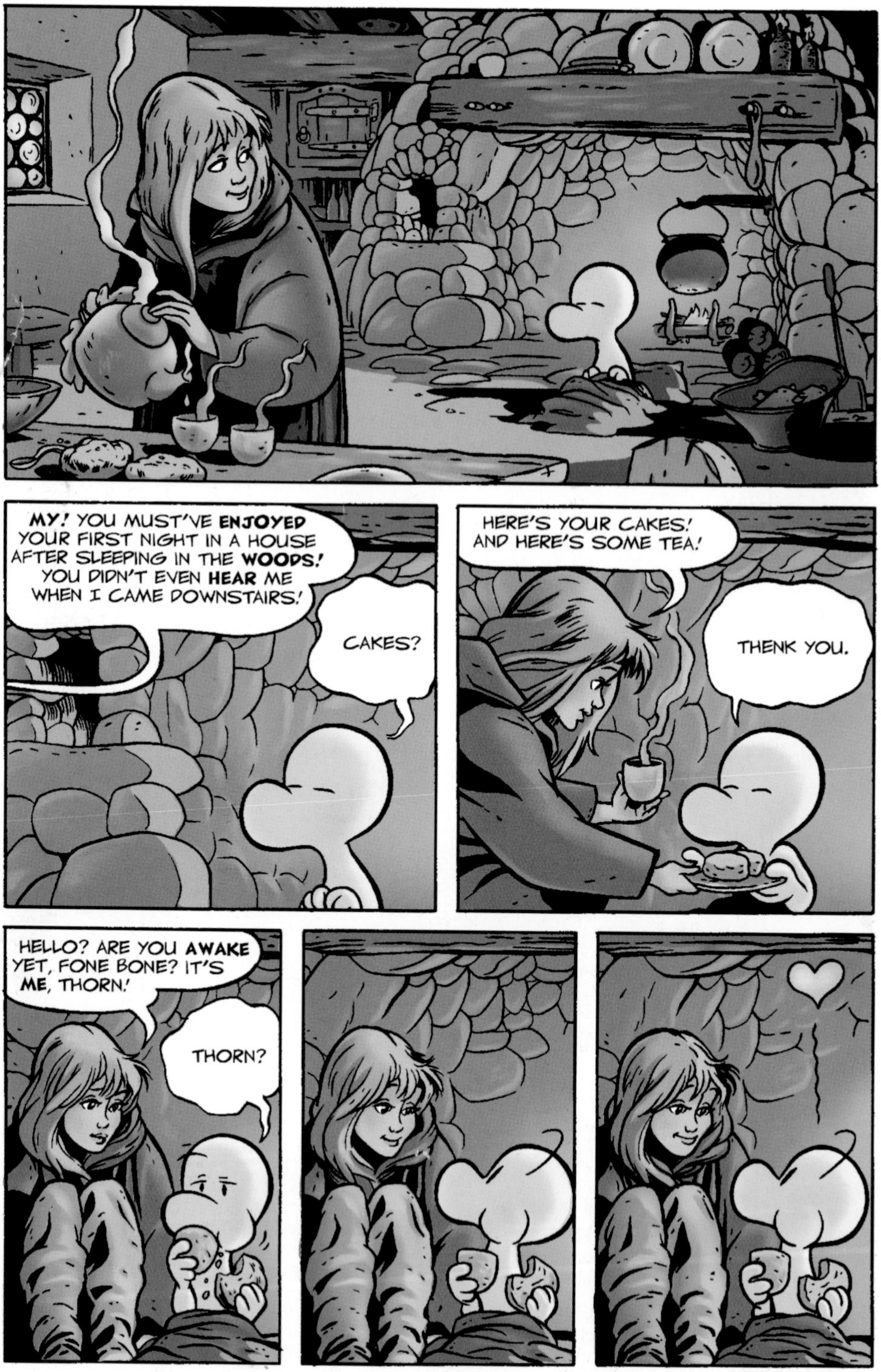
MY! YOU MUST'VE ENJOYED YOUR FIRST NIGHT IN A HOUSE AFTER SLEEPING IN THE WOODS! YOU DIDN'T EVEN HEAR ME WHEN I CAME DOWNSTAIRS!
CAKES?
HERE'S YOUR CAKES! AND HERE'S SOME TEA!
THENK YOU.
HELLO? ARE YOU AWAKE YET, FONE BONE? IT'S ME, THORN!
THORN?

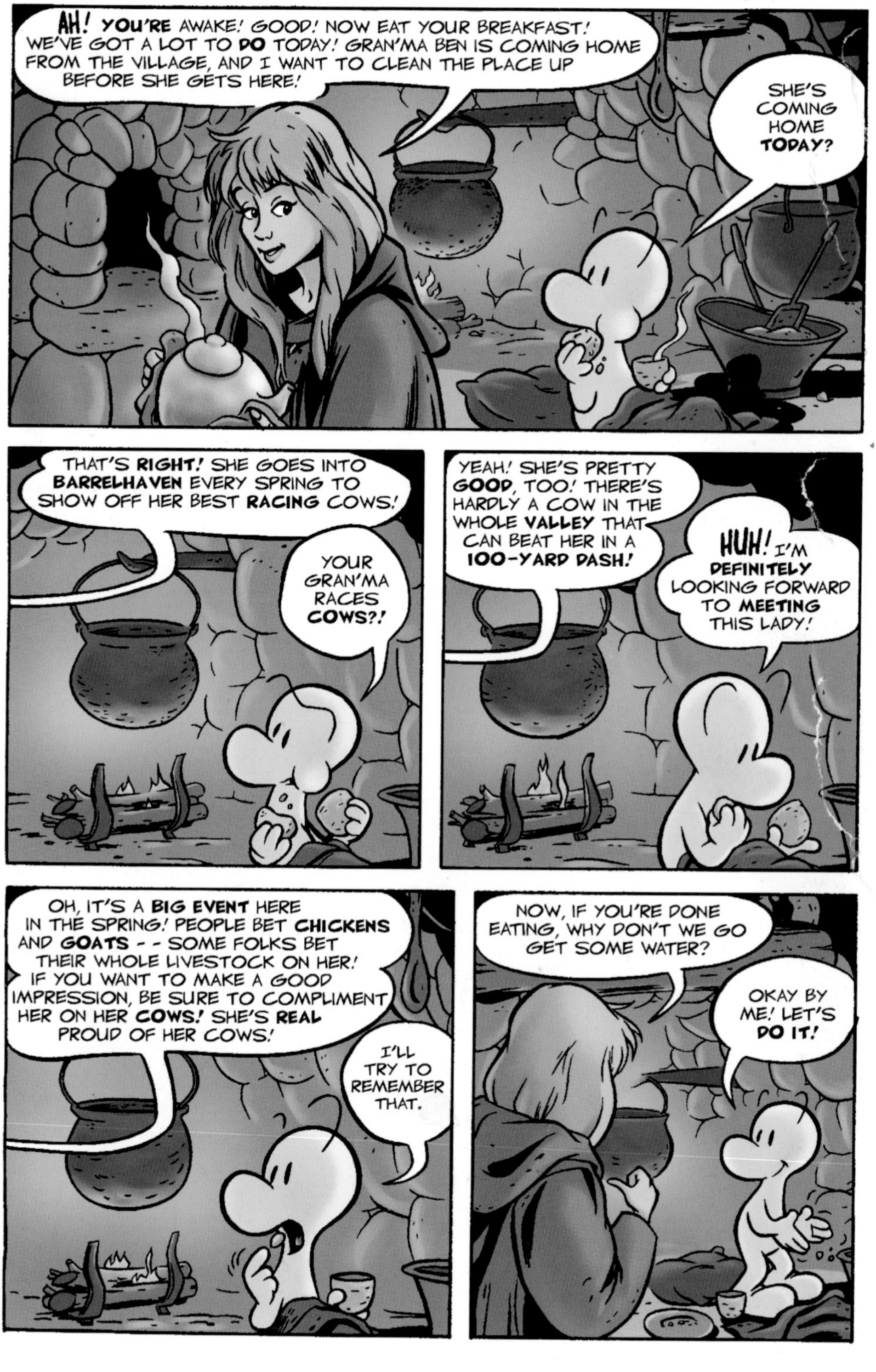
AH! YOU'RE AWAKE! GOOD! NOW EAT YOUR BREAKFAST! WE'VE GOT A LOT TO DO TODAY! GRAN'MA BEN IS COMING HOME FROM THE VILLAGE, AND I WANT TO CLEAN THE PLACE UP BEFORE SHE GETS HERE!
SHE'S COMING HOME TODAY?
THAT'S RIGHT! SHE GOES INTO BARRELHAVEN EVERY SPRING TO SHOW OFF HER BEST RACING COWS!
YOUR GRAN'MA RACES COWS?!
YEAH! SHE'S PRETTY GOOD, TOO! THERE'S HARDLY A COW IN THE WHOLE VALLEY THAT CAN BEAT HER IN A 100-YARD DASH!
HUH! I'M DEFINITELY LOOKING FORWARD TO MEETING THIS LADY!
OH, IT'S A BIG EVENT HERE IN THE SPRING! PEOPLE BET CHICKENS AND GOATS - - SOME FOLKS BET THEIR WHOLE LIVESTOCK ON HER! IF YOU WANT TO MAKE A GOOD IMPRESSION, BE SURE TO COMPLIMENT HER ON HER COWS! SHE'S REAL PROUD OF HER COWS!
I'LL TRY TO REMEMBER THAT.
NOW, IF YOU'RE DONE EATING, WHY DON'T WE GO GET SOME WATER?
OKAY BY ME! LET'S DO IT!

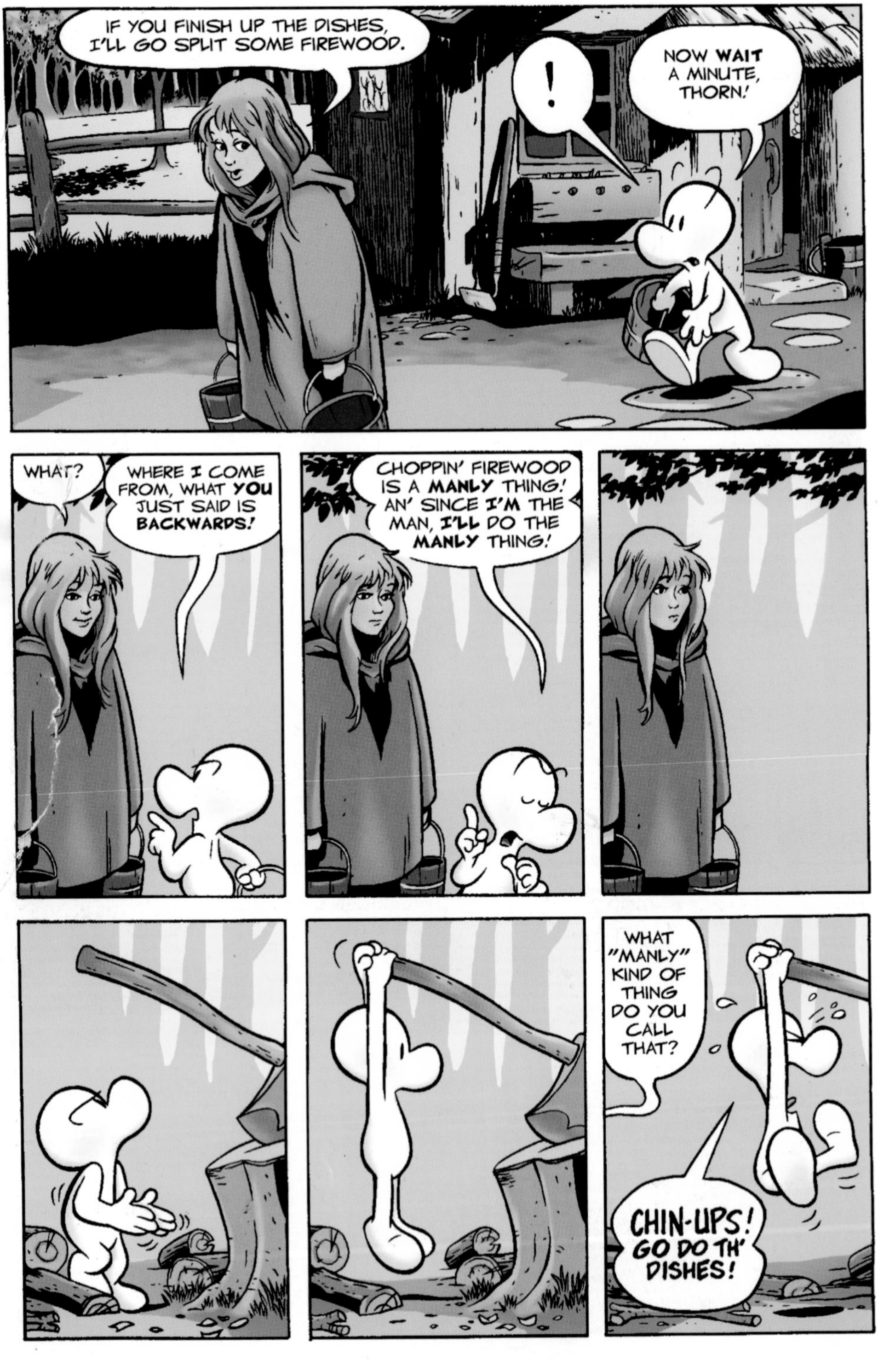
IF YOU FINISH UP THE DISHES, I'LL GO SPLIT SOME FIREWOOD.
!
NOW WAIT A MINUTE, THORN!
WHAT?
WHERE I COME FROM, WHAT YOU JUST SAID IS BACKWARDS!
CHOPPIN' FIREWOOD IS A MANLY THING! AN' SINCE I'M THE MAN, I'LL DO THE MANLY THING!
WHAT "MANLY" KIND OF THING DO YOU CALL THAT?
CHIN-UPS! GO DO TH' DISHES!

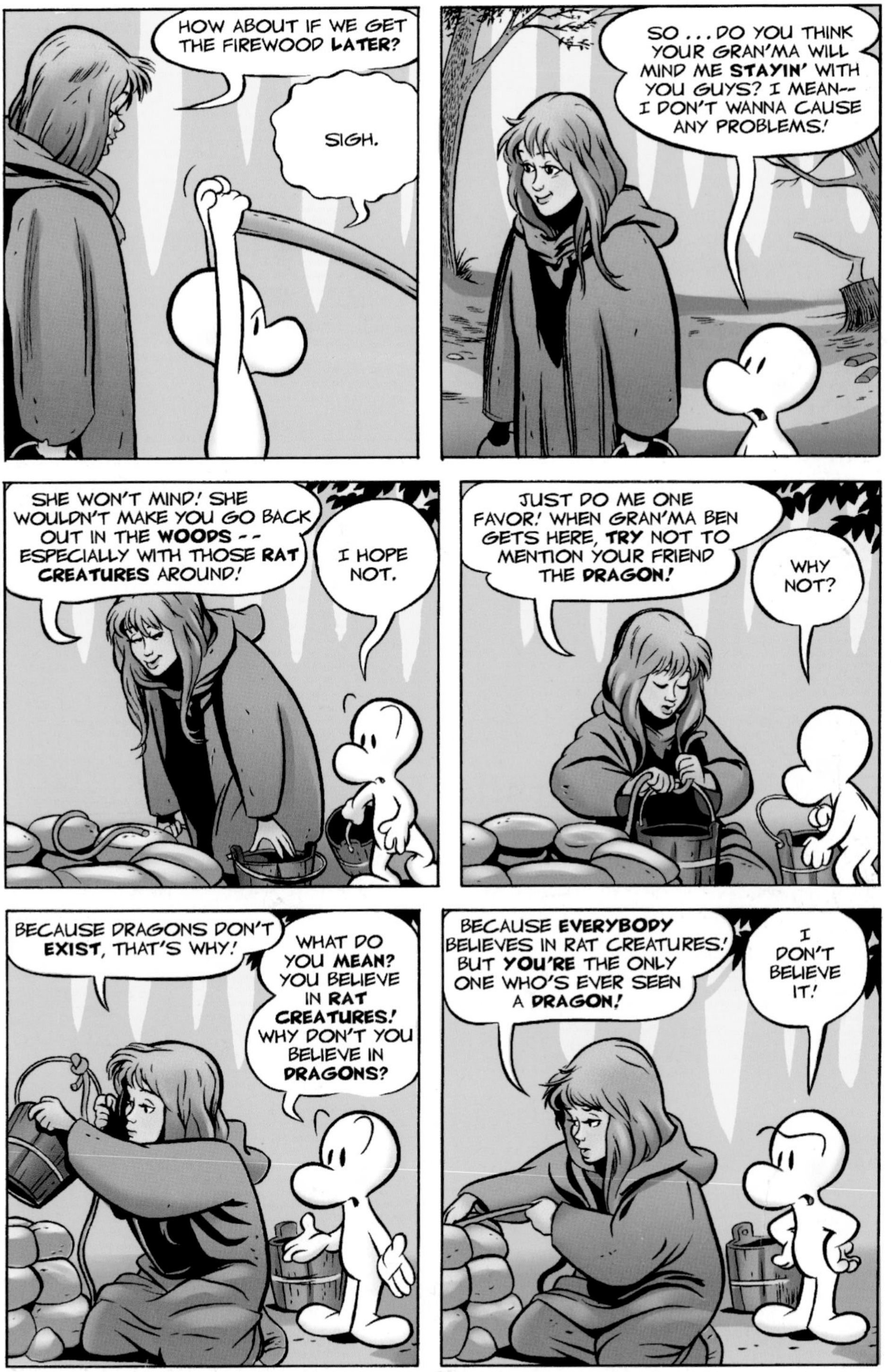
HOW ABOUT IF WE GET THE FIREWOOD **LATER?**
SIGH.
SO . . . DO YOU THINK YOUR GRAN'MA WILL MIND ME **STAYIN'** WITH YOU GUYS? I MEAN-- I DON'T WANNA CAUSE ANY PROBLEMS!
SHE WON'T MIND! SHE WOULDN'T MAKE YOU GO BACK OUT IN THE **WOODS** -- ESPECIALLY WITH THOSE **RAT CREATURES** AROUND!
I HOPE NOT.
JUST DO ME ONE FAVOR! WHEN GRAN'MA BEN GETS HERE, **TRY** NOT TO MENTION YOUR FRIEND THE **DRAGON!**
WHY NOT?
BECAUSE DRAGONS DON'T **EXIST**, THAT'S WHY!
WHAT DO YOU **MEAN?** YOU BELIEVE IN **RAT CREATURES!** WHY DON'T YOU BELIEVE IN **DRAGONS?**
BECAUSE **EVERYBODY** BELIEVES IN RAT CREATURES! BUT **YOU'RE** THE ONLY ONE WHO'S EVER SEEN A **DRAGON!**
I DON'T BELIEVE IT!

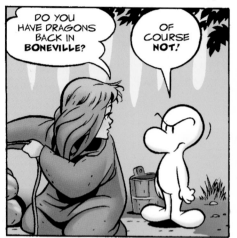

DO YOU HAVE DRAGONS BACK IN **BONEVILLE?**

OF COURSE **NOT.'**

WELL?

WELL, WE DON'T HAVE BIGMOUTHED, DROOLING, **RAT-LIKE** MONSTERS, EITHER! UNLESS YOU COUNT MY COUSIN **PHONEY BONE!**

AN' YOU KNOW WHAT **ELSE?** I THINK THAT DRAGON IS FOLLOWIN' ME **AROUND!**

FONE BONE! WE'VE BEEN OVER THIS A HUNDRED TIMES!

BUT I'M TELLIN' YA, I **SAW** ONE! HE HAD A GOATEE, 'N' A CIGARETTE, 'N' BIG OL' HAIRY EARS LIKE **THIS!**

DRAGONS ARE MAKE-BELIEVE! YOU WERE SEEING THINGS!

THANKS FOR THE SUPPORT, THORN! YOU KNOW, THAT'S WHAT THE DRAGON **WANTS** YOU TO THINK! HE DOESN'T WANT YOU TO KNOW HE **EXISTS!**

ACTUALLY, I JUST WANT HER TO THINK YOU'RE **NUTS!**

OH, SHUT **UP!**

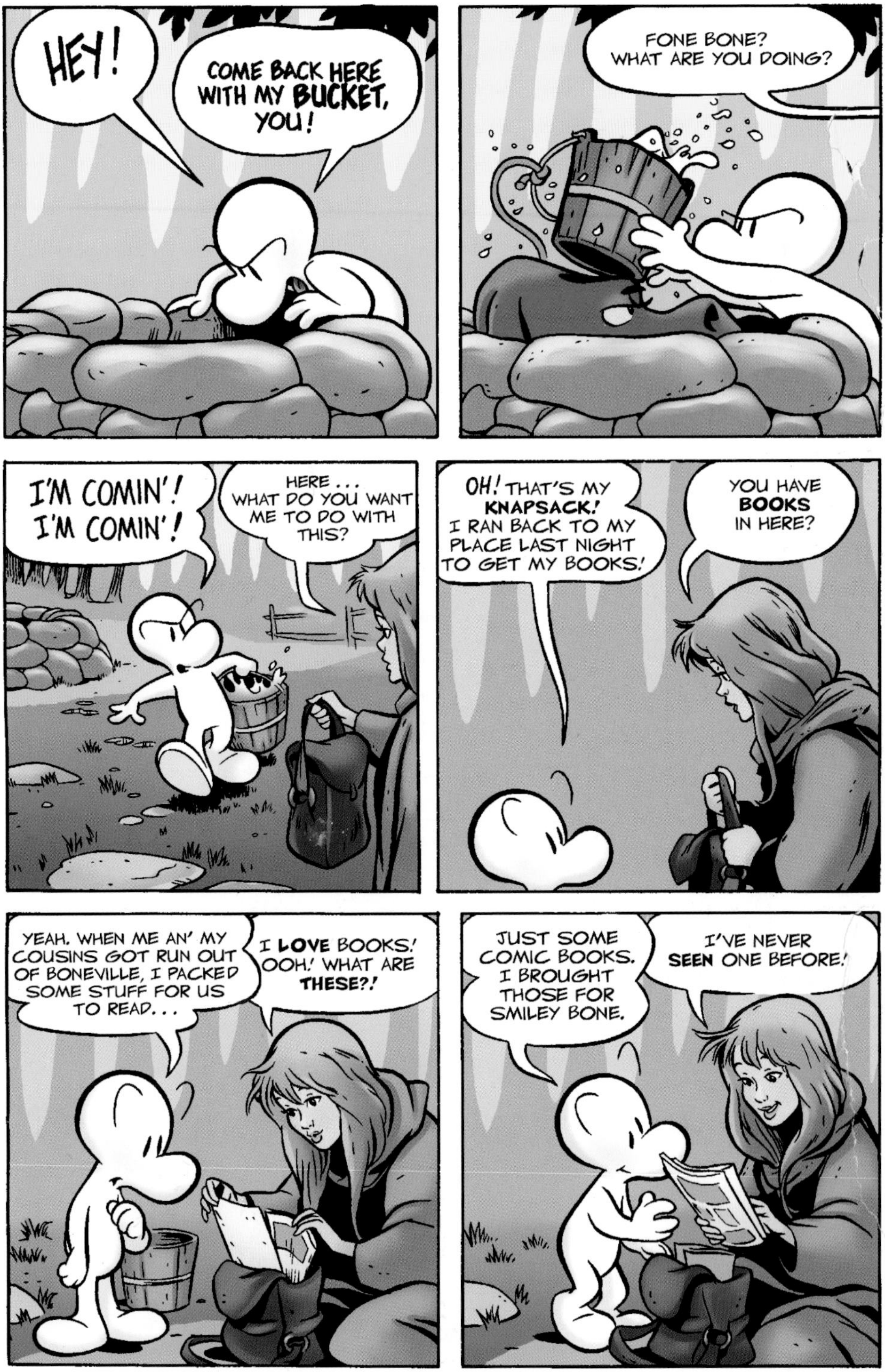
HEY!
COME BACK HERE WITH MY BUCKET, YOU!
FONE BONE? WHAT ARE YOU DOING?
I'M COMIN'! I'M COMIN'!
HERE... WHAT DO YOU WANT ME TO DO WITH THIS?
OH! THAT'S MY KNAPSACK! I RAN BACK TO MY PLACE LAST NIGHT TO GET MY BOOKS!
YOU HAVE BOOKS IN HERE?
YEAH. WHEN ME AN' MY COUSINS GOT RUN OUT OF BONEVILLE, I PACKED SOME STUFF FOR US TO READ...
I LOVE BOOKS! OOH! WHAT ARE THESE?!
JUST SOME COMIC BOOKS. I BROUGHT THOSE FOR SMILEY BONE.
I'VE NEVER SEEN ONE BEFORE!

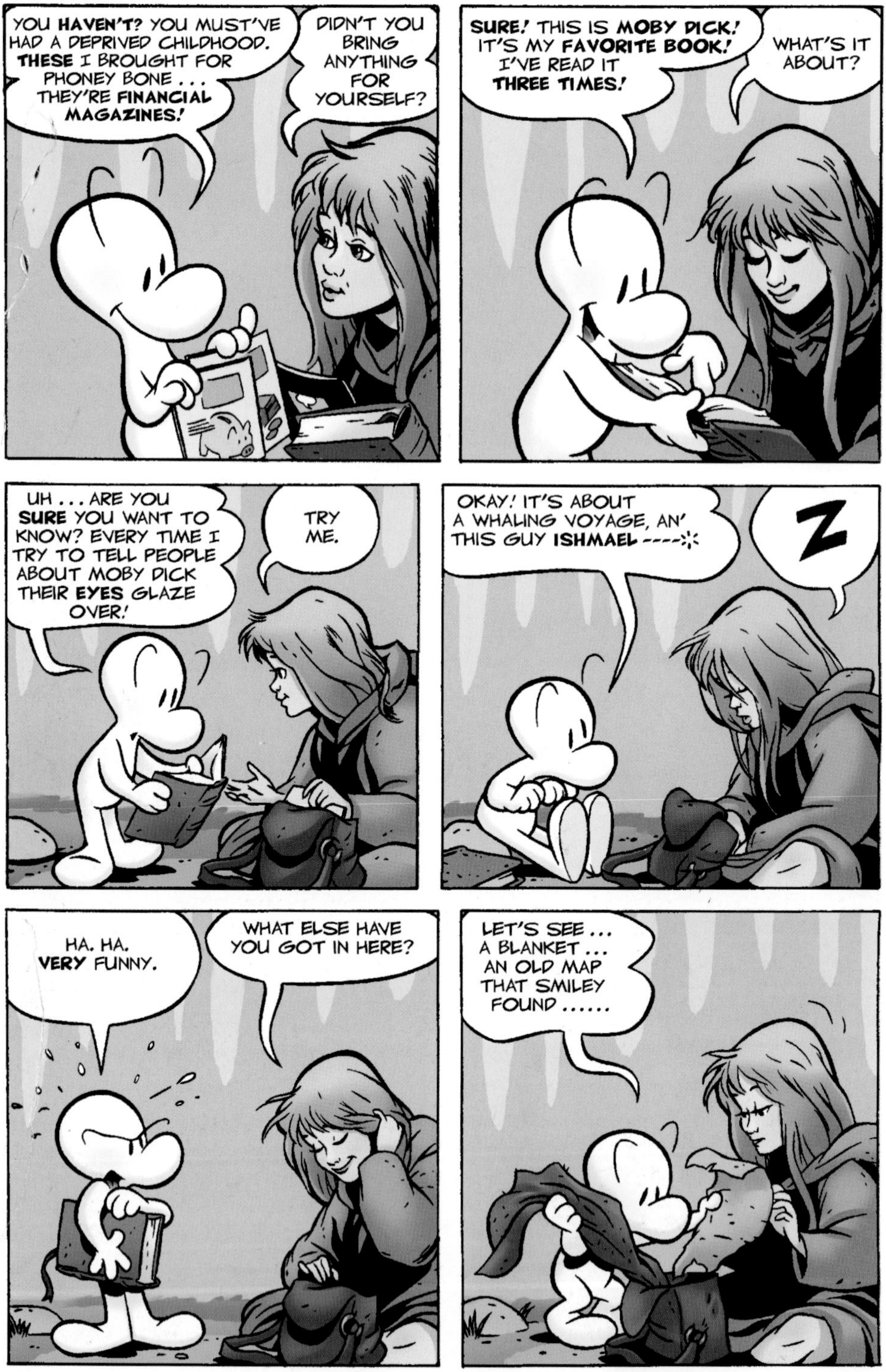
YOU HAVEN'T? YOU MUST'VE HAD A DEPRIVED CHILDHOOD. THESE I BROUGHT FOR PHONEY BONE ... THEY'RE FINANCIAL MAGAZINES!
DIDN'T YOU BRING ANYTHING FOR YOURSELF?
SURE! THIS IS MOBY DICK! IT'S MY FAVORITE BOOK! I'VE READ IT THREE TIMES!
WHAT'S IT ABOUT?
UH ... ARE YOU SURE YOU WANT TO KNOW? EVERY TIME I TRY TO TELL PEOPLE ABOUT MOBY DICK THEIR EYES GLAZE OVER!
TRY ME.
OKAY! IT'S ABOUT A WHALING VOYAGE, AN' THIS GUY ISHMAEL ----
Z
HA. HA. VERY FUNNY.
WHAT ELSE HAVE YOU GOT IN HERE?
LET'S SEE ... A BLANKET ... AN OLD MAP THAT SMILEY FOUND ......

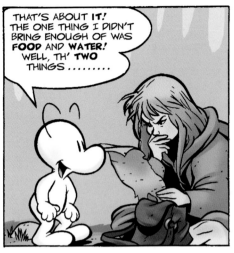

THAT'S ABOUT **IT!** THE ONE THING I DIDN'T BRING ENOUGH OF WAS **FOOD** AND **WATER!** WELL, TH' **TWO** THINGS ....

WHY ARE YOU MAKING THAT FACE?

I DON'T KNOW .... SOMETHING ABOUT THIS MAP IS FAMILIAR ...

REALLY? SMILEY FOUND IT OUT IN TH' DESERT RIGHT BEFORE WE GOT SPLIT UP.

IT REMINDS ME OF A DREAM I USED TO HAVE ...

WHOA. AND YOU THINK **MY** STORIES ARE STRANGE!

ARE YOU OKAY?

I'M FINE, LET'S JUST FORGET IT. C'MON, GRAN'MA WILL BE HERE SOON ...

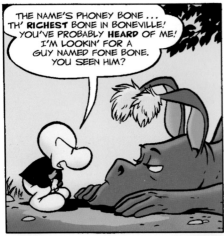

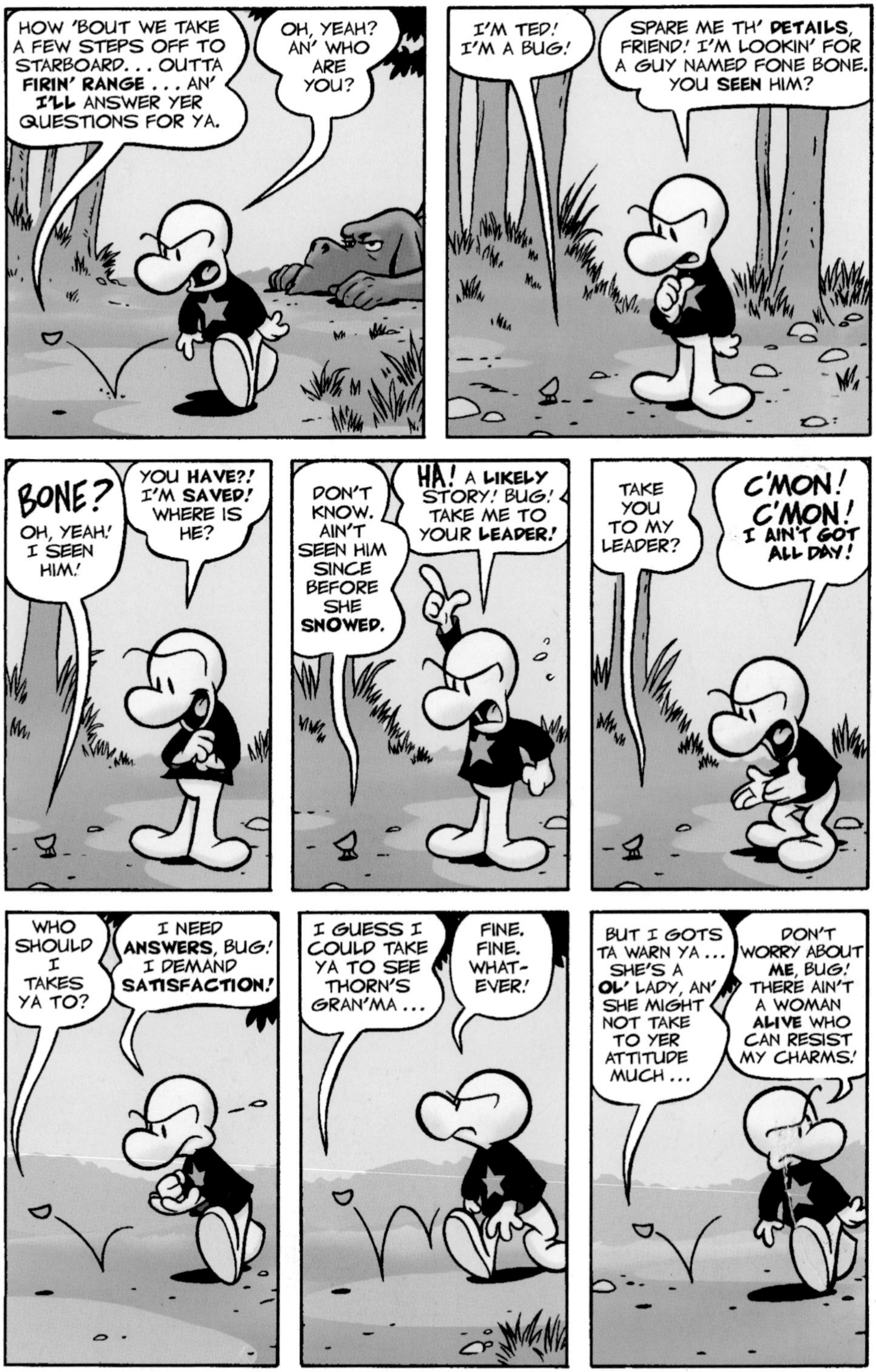
HOW 'BOUT WE TAKE A FEW STEPS OFF TO STARBOARD. . . OUTTA FIRIN' RANGE . . . AN' I'LL ANSWER YER QUESTIONS FOR YA.
OH, YEAH? AN' WHO ARE YOU?
I'M TED! I'M A BUG!
SPARE ME TH' DETAILS, FRIEND! I'M LOOKIN' FOR A GUY NAMED FONE BONE. YOU SEEN HIM?
BONE? OH, YEAH! I SEEN HIM!
YOU HAVE?! I'M SAVED! WHERE IS HE?
DON'T KNOW. AIN'T SEEN HIM SINCE BEFORE SHE SNOWED.
HA! A LIKELY STORY! BUG! TAKE ME TO YOUR LEADER!
TAKE YOU TO MY LEADER?
C'MON! C'MON! I AIN'T GOT ALL DAY!
WHO SHOULD I TAKES YA TO?
I NEED ANSWERS, BUG! I DEMAND SATISFACTION!
I GUESS I COULD TAKE YA TO SEE THORN'S GRAN'MA . . .
FINE. FINE. WHAT-EVER!
BUT I GOTS TA WARN YA . . . SHE'S A OL' LADY, AN' SHE MIGHT NOT TAKE TO YER ATTITUDE MUCH . . .
DON'T WORRY ABOUT ME, BUG! THERE AIN'T A WOMAN ALIVE WHO CAN RESIST MY CHARMS!

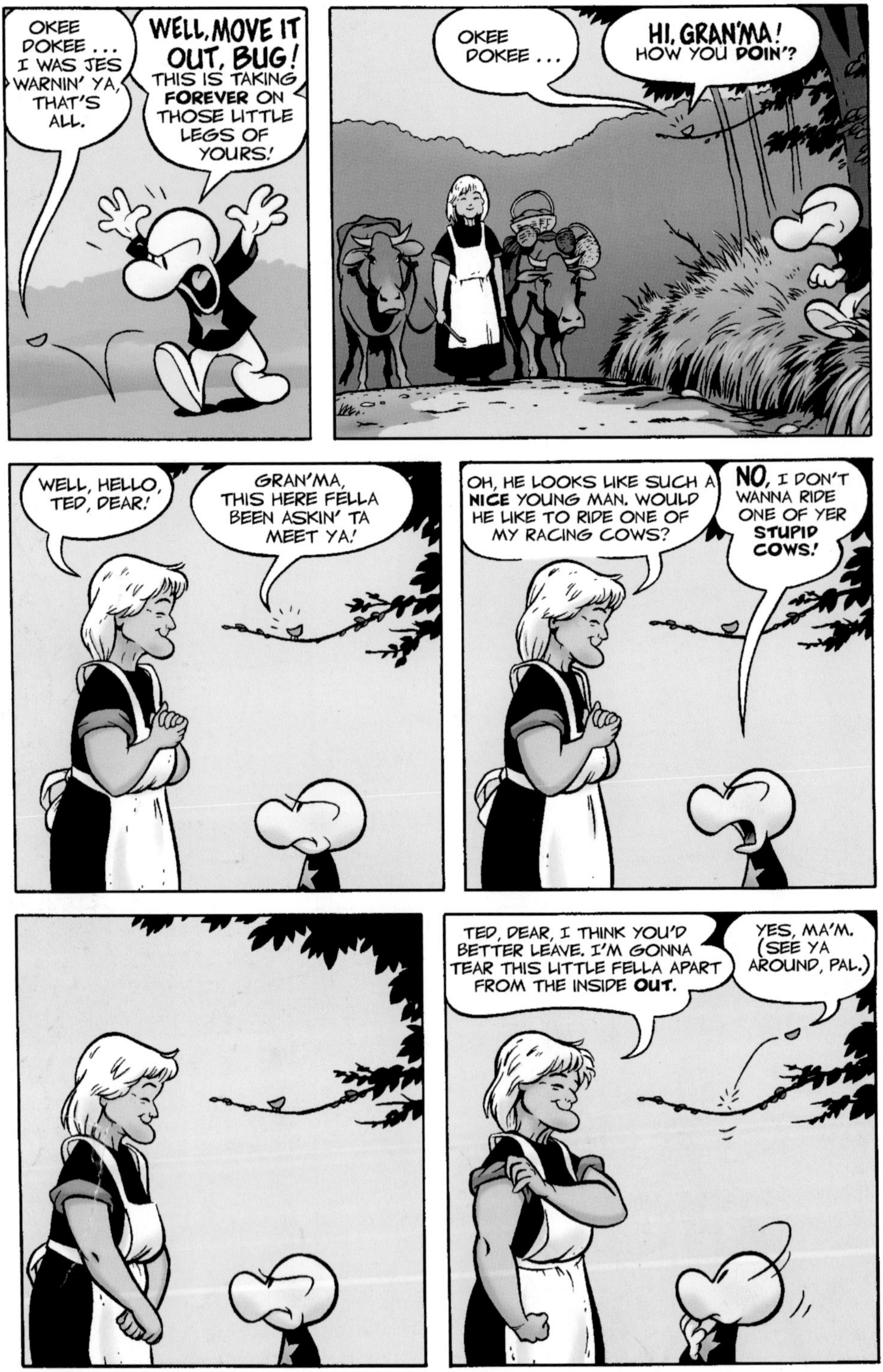
OKEE DOKEE ... I WAS JES WARNIN' YA, THAT'S ALL.
WELL, MOVE IT OUT, BUG! THIS IS TAKING FOREVER ON THOSE LITTLE LEGS OF YOURS!
OKEE DOKEE ...
HI, GRAN'MA! HOW YOU DOIN'?
WELL, HELLO, TED, DEAR!
GRAN'MA, THIS HERE FELLA BEEN ASKIN' TA MEET YA!
OH, HE LOOKS LIKE SUCH A NICE YOUNG MAN. WOULD HE LIKE TO RIDE ONE OF MY RACING COWS?
NO, I DON'T WANNA RIDE ONE OF YER STUPID COWS!
TED, DEAR, I THINK YOU'D BETTER LEAVE. I'M GONNA TEAR THIS LITTLE FELLA APART FROM THE INSIDE OUT.
YES, MA'M. (SEE YA AROUND, PAL.)

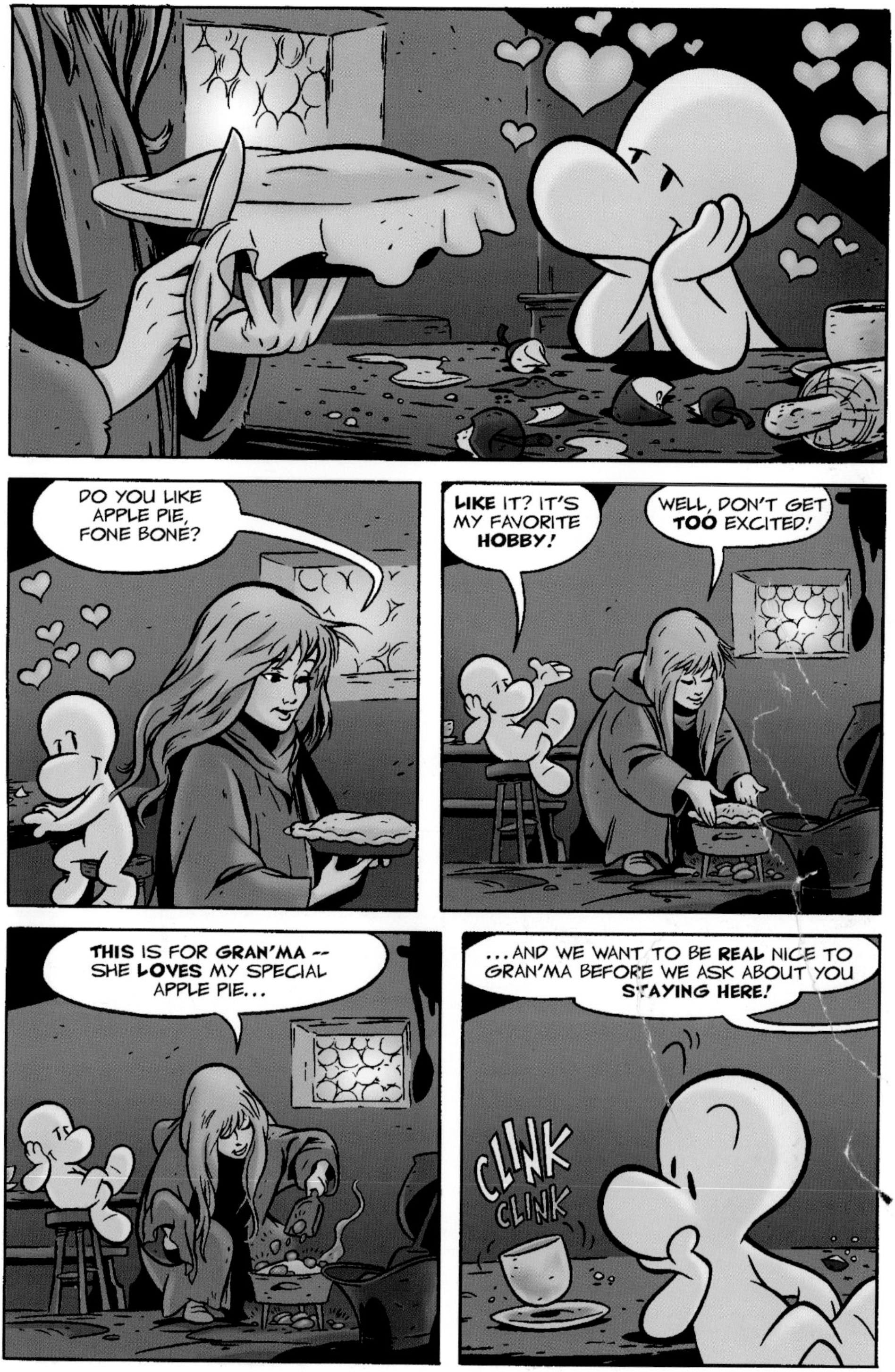
DO YOU LIKE APPLE PIE, FONE BONE?
LIKE IT? IT'S MY FAVORITE HOBBY!
WELL, DON'T GET TOO EXCITED!
THIS IS FOR GRAN'MA -- SHE LOVES MY SPECIAL APPLE PIE...
...AND WE WANT TO BE REAL NICE TO GRAN'MA BEFORE WE ASK ABOUT YOU STAYING HERE!
CLINK
CLINK

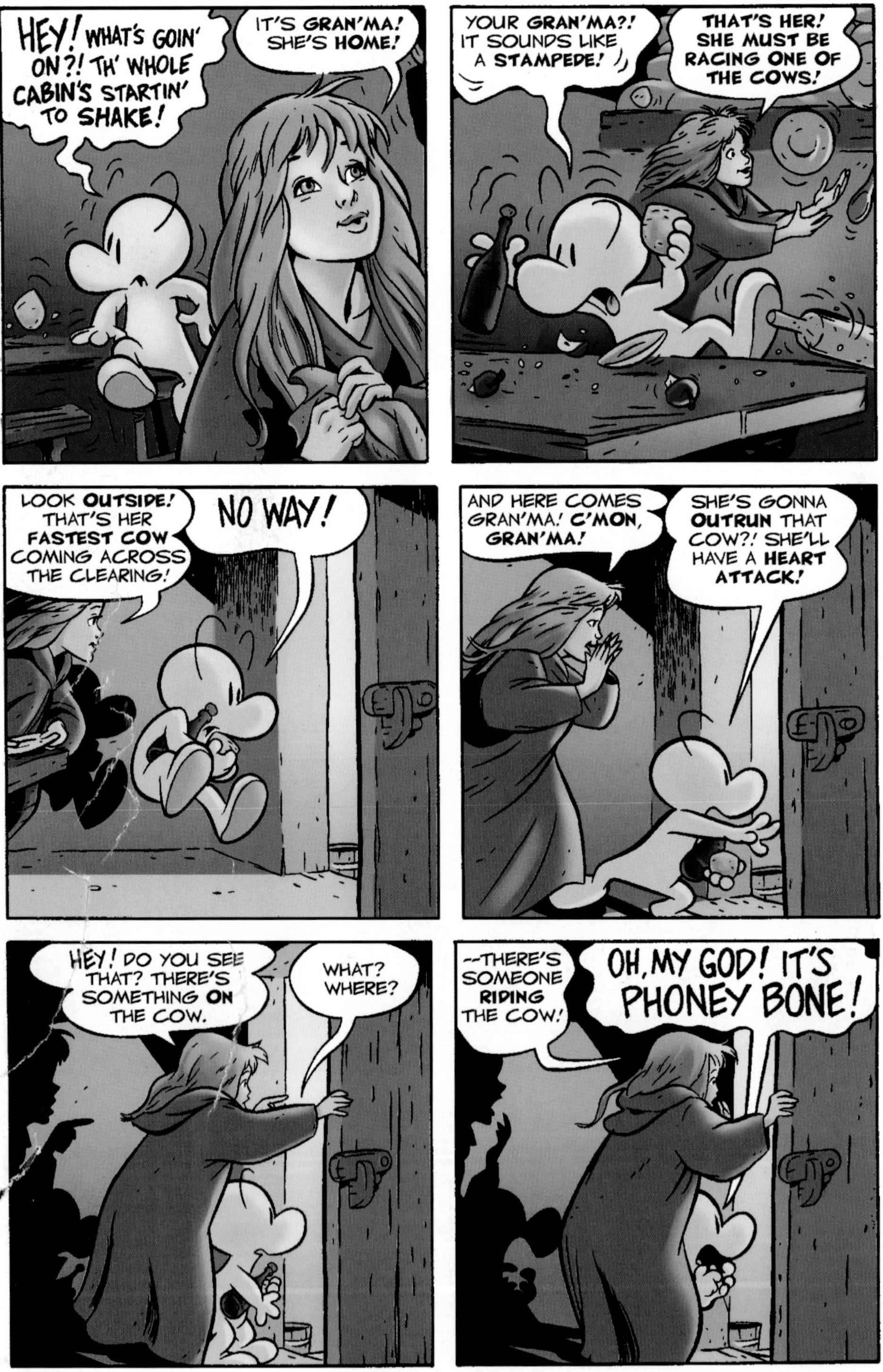
HEY! WHAT'S GOIN' ON?! TH' WHOLE CABIN'S STARTIN' TO SHAKE!
IT'S GRAN'MA! SHE'S HOME!
YOUR GRAN'MA?! IT SOUNDS LIKE A STAMPEDE!
THAT'S HER! SHE MUST BE RACING ONE OF THE COWS!
LOOK OUTSIDE! THAT'S HER FASTEST COW COMING ACROSS THE CLEARING!
NO WAY!
AND HERE COMES GRAN'MA! C'MON, GRAN'MA!
SHE'S GONNA OUTRUN THAT COW?! SHE'LL HAVE A HEART ATTACK!
HEY! DO YOU SEE THAT? THERE'S SOMETHING ON THE COW.
WHAT? WHERE?
--THERE'S SOMEONE RIDING THE COW!
OH, MY GOD! IT'S PHONEY BONE!

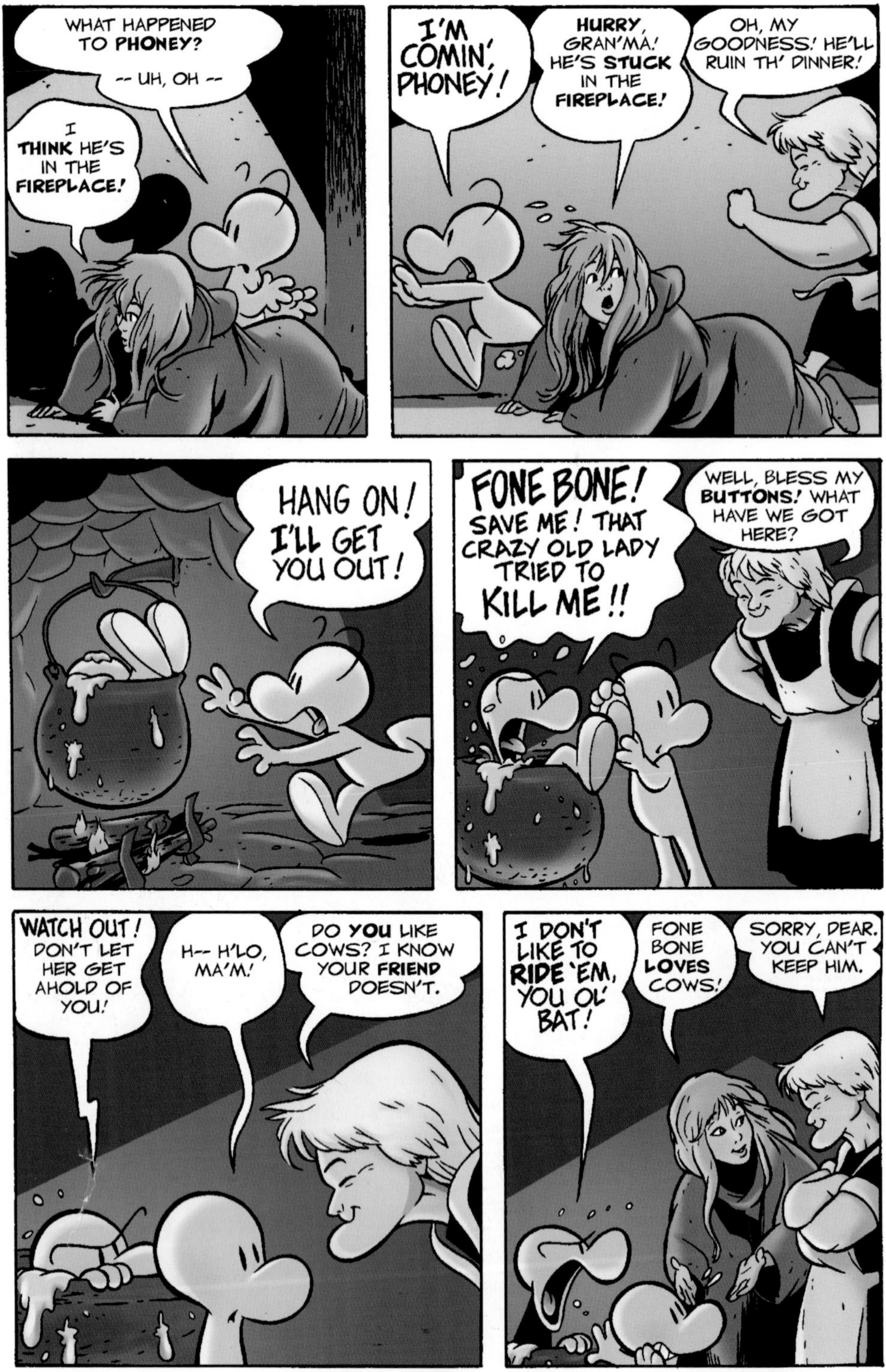
WHAT HAPPENED TO PHONEY?
-- UH, OH --
I THINK HE'S IN THE FIREPLACE!
I'M COMIN', PHONEY!
HURRY, GRAN'MA! HE'S STUCK IN THE FIREPLACE!
OH, MY GOODNESS! HE'LL RUIN TH' DINNER!
HANG ON! I'LL GET YOU OUT!
FONE BONE! SAVE ME! THAT CRAZY OLD LADY TRIED TO KILL ME!!
WELL, BLESS MY BUTTONS! WHAT HAVE WE GOT HERE?
WATCH OUT! DON'T LET HER GET AHOLD OF YOU!
H-- H'LO, MA'M!
DO YOU LIKE COWS? I KNOW YOUR FRIEND DOESN'T.
I DON'T LIKE TO RIDE 'EM, YOU OL' BAT!
FONE BONE LOVES COWS!
SORRY, DEAR. YOU CAN'T KEEP HIM.

BUT--

NO BUTS. I DON'T WANT ANY PETS RUNNING AROUND TH' HOUSE.

GRAN'MA! THEY'RE NOT PETS!

CAN YOU MILK 'EM? IF YOU CAN'T MILK 'EM, THEY'RE PETS!

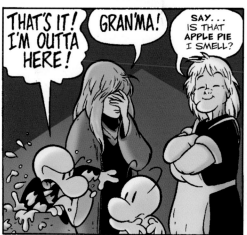

THAT'S IT! I'M OUTTA HERE!

GRAN'MA!

SAY... IS THAT APPLE PIE I SMELL?

YES! I BAKED ONE OF MY SPECIAL PIES JUST FOR YOU!

WHAT A SWEET THING YOU ARE!

QUICK! WHILE SHE'S DISTRACTED!

HOLD IT! THORN THINKS GRAN'MA BEN CAN HELP US GET BACK TO BONEVILLE!

IT'S NOT WORTH IT! LET GO OF ME!

WOULD YOU WAIT A MINUTE?!! WE CAN EXPLAIN EVERYTHING!

HELP! HELP! THEY'VE DESTROYED MY COUSIN'S BRAIN!! OH, MY GOD! THEY'VE ALREADY MILKED YOU, HAVEN'T THEY?!!

GRAN'MA, THEY'RE **BONES!** THEY COME FROM A PLACE CALLED BONEVILLE! AND THEY NEED OUR HELP TO GET **BACK!**

WHERE'S SMILEY?

SMILEY? I THOUGHT HE WAS WITH **YOU!**

YOU HAVEN'T SEEN HIM SINCE WE SPLIT UP? BUT I **KNOW** HE'S IN TH' VALLEY! I FOUND ONE OF HIS **CIGAR BUTTS!**

TH' LAST TIME I SAW THAT CHOWDERHEAD, HE WAS SAYIN' HOW **COOL** IT WAS THAT WE WERE ABOUT TO BE PULVERIZED BY INSECTS!

YEAH! THAT'S TH' LAST TIME **I** SAW HIM, TOO...

AW, QUIT YER **WORRYIN'!** WHY DON'T YA INTRODUCE ME TO YER GOOD-LOOKIN' FRIEND, HERE?

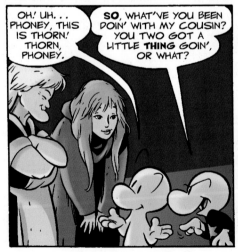

OH! UH... PHONEY, THIS IS THORN! THORN, PHONEY.

SO, WHAT'VE YOU BEEN DOIN' WITH MY COUSIN? YOU TWO GOT A LITTLE **THING** GOIN', OR WHAT?

PHONEY!

NO, HUH? FIGURES! WHAT'D YA **DO? BORE** HER TO DEATH TALKIN' ABOUT **MOBY DICK?**

I'M GOING TO BED. YOU CAN KEEP 'EM IF YOU WANT, BUT THEY HAVE TO SLEEP IN TH' BARN.

GRAM!

G'NIGHT MA'M IT WAS NICE MEETING YOU!

FONE BONE, COULD I TALK TO YOU FOR A MOMENT? OUTSIDE?

YES.

WELL, GO AHEAD! I AIN'T STOPPIN' YA!

THIS ISN'T GOING QUITE THE WAY WE **PLANNED**, IS IT? TELL ME... IS HE **ALWAYS** LIKE THIS?

PRETTY MUCH.

HMM. GRAN'MA'S GOING BACK TO **BARRELHAVEN** IN A FEW DAYS FOR THE SPRING FESTIVAL. IF WE CAN JUST KEEP THOSE TWO **CALM** UNTIL **THEN**, WE CAN ALL GO INTO TOWN TOGETHER TO LOOK FOR YOUR OTHER COUSIN.

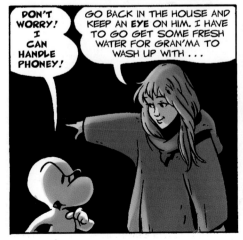

DON'T WORRY! I CAN HANDLE PHONEY!

GO BACK IN THE HOUSE AND KEEP AN **EYE** ON HIM. I HAVE TO GO GET SOME FRESH WATER FOR GRAN'MA TO WASH UP WITH...

OKAY, PHONEY! WE HAVE TO GET A COUPLE OF THINGS STRAIGHT---

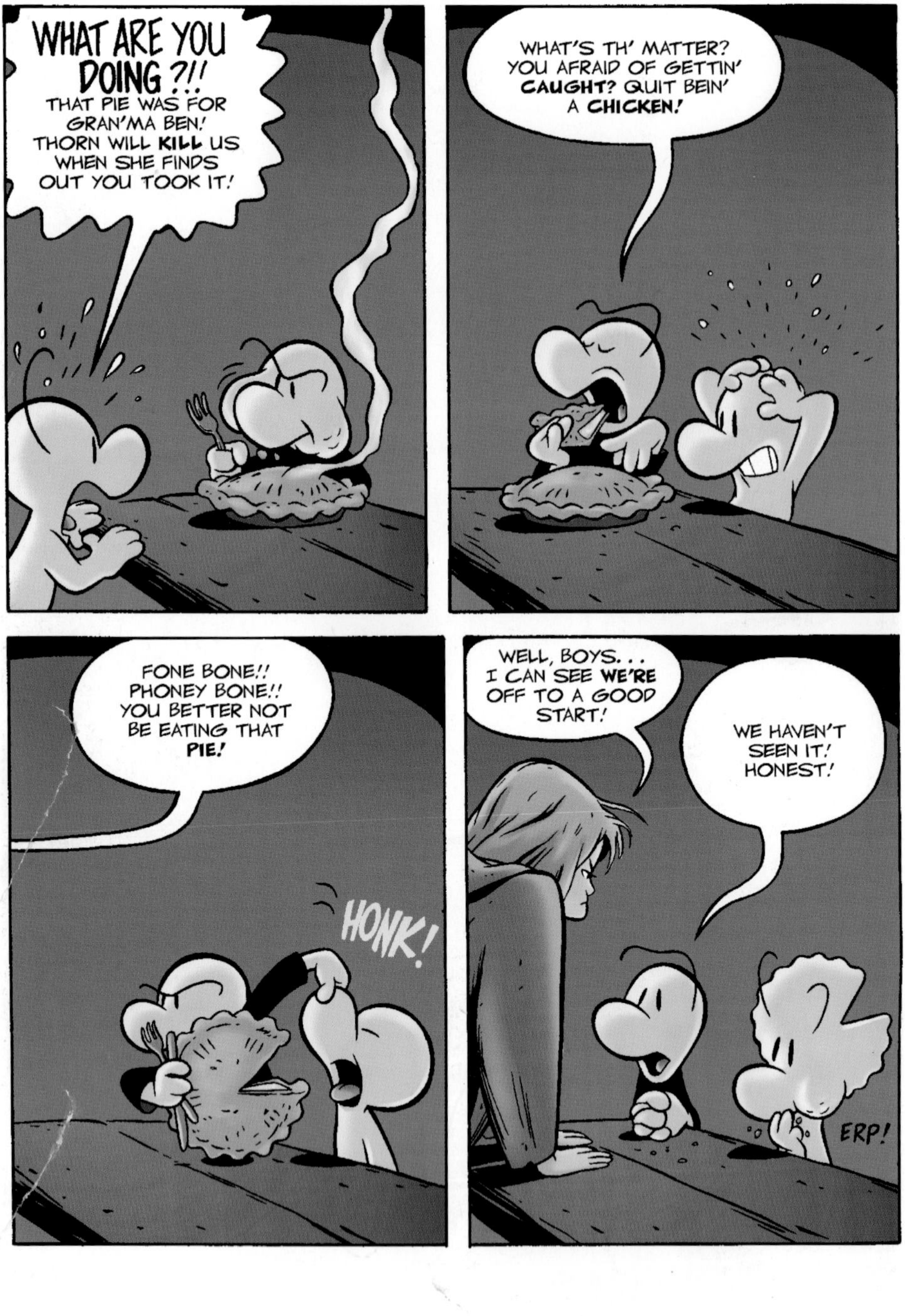
WHAT ARE YOU DOING ?!!... THAT PIE WAS FOR GRAN'MA BEN! THORN WILL KILL US WHEN SHE FINDS OUT YOU TOOK IT!
WHAT'S TH' MATTER? YOU AFRAID OF GETTIN' CAUGHT? QUIT BEIN' A CHICKEN!
FONE BONE!! PHONEY BONE!! YOU BETTER NOT BE EATING THAT PIE!
HONK!
WELL, BOYS. . . I CAN SEE WE'RE OFF TO A GOOD START!
WE HAVEN'T SEEN IT! HONEST!
ERP!

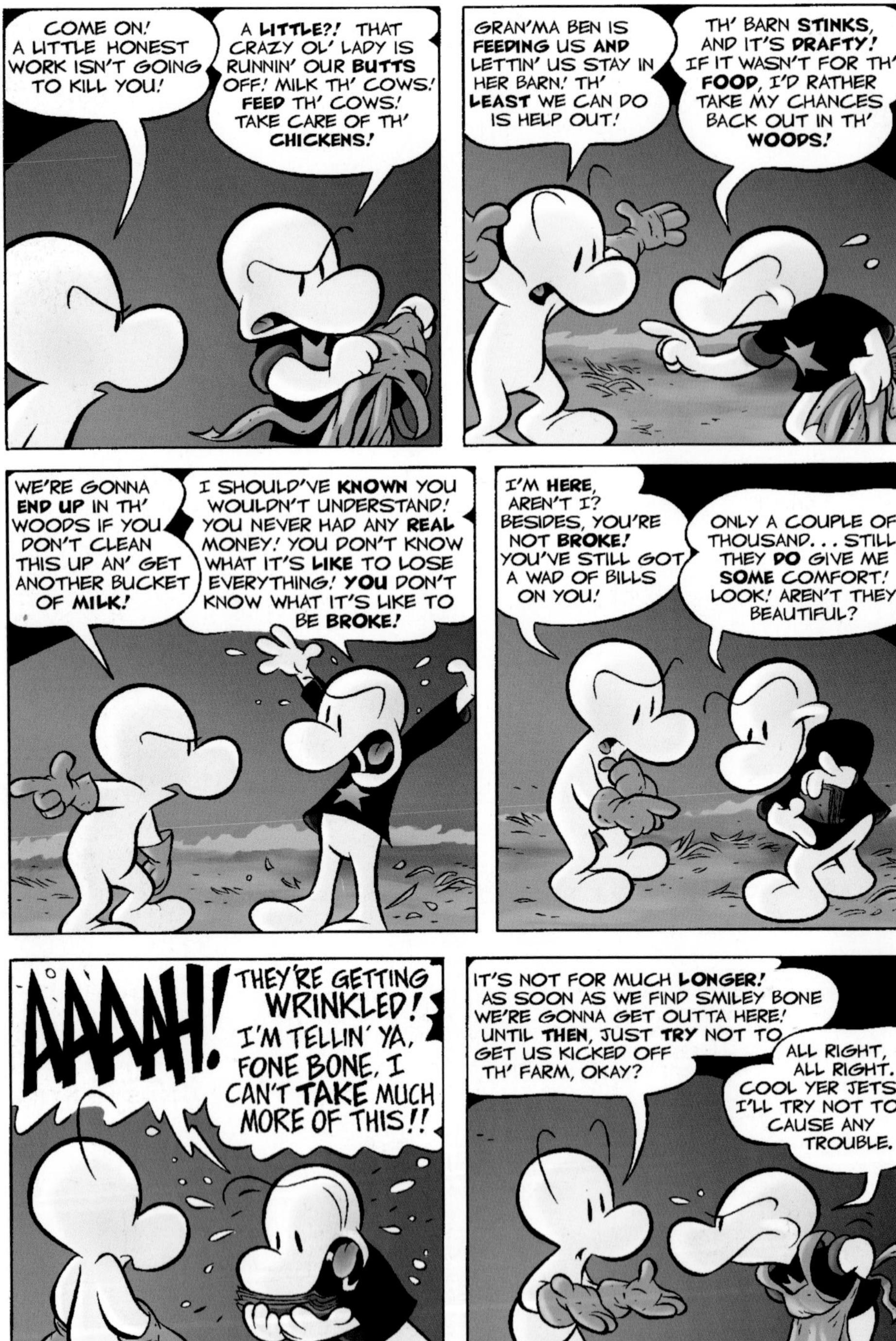
COME ON! A LITTLE HONEST WORK ISN'T GOING TO KILL YOU!
A LITTLE?! THAT CRAZY OL' LADY IS RUNNIN' OUR BUTTS OFF! MILK TH' COWS! FEED TH' COWS! TAKE CARE OF TH' CHICKENS!
GRAN'MA BEN IS FEEDING US AND LETTIN' US STAY IN HER BARN! TH' LEAST WE CAN DO IS HELP OUT!
TH' BARN STINKS, AND IT'S DRAFTY! IF IT WASN'T FOR TH' FOOD, I'D RATHER TAKE MY CHANCES BACK OUT IN TH' WOODS!
WE'RE GONNA END UP IN TH' WOODS IF YOU DON'T CLEAN THIS UP AN' GET ANOTHER BUCKET OF MILK!
I SHOULD'VE KNOWN YOU WOULDN'T UNDERSTAND! YOU NEVER HAD ANY REAL MONEY! YOU DON'T KNOW WHAT IT'S LIKE TO LOSE EVERYTHING! YOU DON'T KNOW WHAT IT'S LIKE TO BE BROKE!
I'M HERE, AREN'T I? BESIDES, YOU'RE NOT BROKE! YOU'VE STILL GOT A WAD OF BILLS ON YOU!
ONLY A COUPLE OF THOUSAND. . . STILL, THEY DO GIVE ME SOME COMFORT! LOOK! AREN'T THEY BEAUTIFUL?
AAAAH!
THEY'RE GETTING WRINKLED! I'M TELLIN' YA, FONE BONE, I CAN'T TAKE MUCH MORE OF THIS!!
IT'S NOT FOR MUCH LONGER! AS SOON AS WE FIND SMILEY BONE WE'RE GONNA GET OUTTA HERE! UNTIL THEN, JUST TRY NOT TO GET US KICKED OFF TH' FARM, OKAY?
ALL RIGHT, ALL RIGHT. COOL YER JETS! I'LL TRY NOT TO CAUSE ANY TROUBLE.

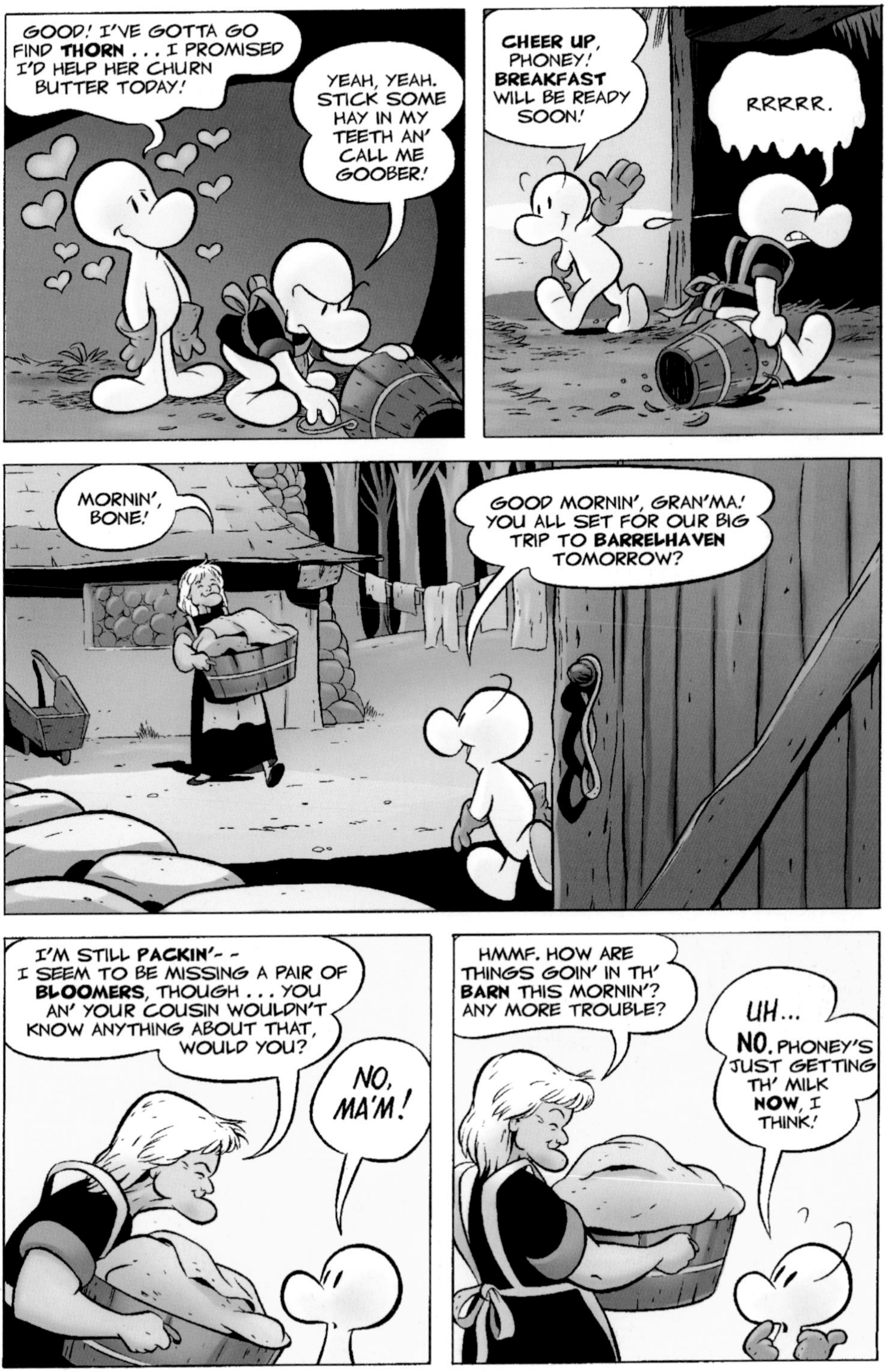
GOOD! I'VE GOTTA GO FIND THORN . . . I PROMISED I'D HELP HER CHURN BUTTER TODAY!
YEAH, YEAH. STICK SOME HAY IN MY TEETH AN' CALL ME GOOBER!
CHEER UP, PHONEY! BREAKFAST WILL BE READY SOON!
RRRRR.
MORNIN', BONE!
GOOD MORNIN', GRAN'MA! YOU ALL SET FOR OUR BIG TRIP TO BARRELHAVEN TOMORROW?
I'M STILL PACKIN'-- I SEEM TO BE MISSING A PAIR OF BLOOMERS, THOUGH . . . YOU AN' YOUR COUSIN WOULDN'T KNOW ANYTHING ABOUT THAT, WOULD YOU?
NO, MA'M!
HMMF. HOW ARE THINGS GOIN' IN TH' BARN THIS MORNIN'? ANY MORE TROUBLE?
UH... NO. PHONEY'S JUST GETTING TH' MILK NOW, I THINK!

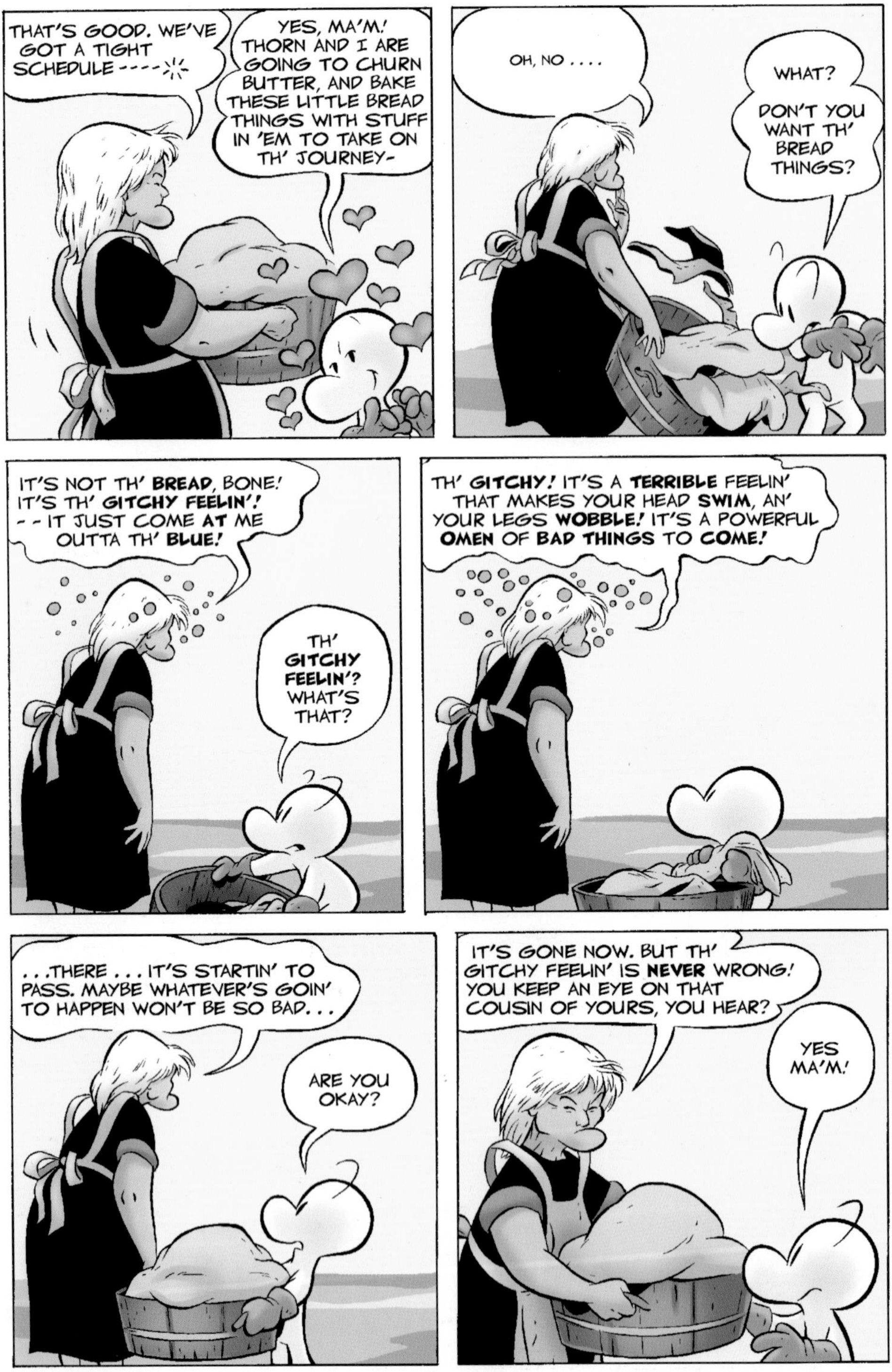
THAT'S GOOD. WE'VE GOT A TIGHT SCHEDULE - - - -
YES, MA'M! THORN AND I ARE GOING TO CHURN BUTTER, AND BAKE THESE LITTLE BREAD THINGS WITH STUFF IN 'EM TO TAKE ON TH' JOURNEY-
OH, NO . . . .
WHAT?
DON'T YOU WANT TH' BREAD THINGS?
IT'S NOT TH' BREAD, BONE! IT'S TH' GITCHY FEELIN'! - - IT JUST COME AT ME OUTTA TH' BLUE!
TH' GITCHY FEELIN'? WHAT'S THAT?
TH' GITCHY! IT'S A TERRIBLE FEELIN' THAT MAKES YOUR HEAD SWIM, AN' YOUR LEGS WOBBLE! IT'S A POWERFUL OMEN OF BAD THINGS TO COME!
. . .THERE . . . IT'S STARTIN' TO PASS. MAYBE WHATEVER'S GOIN' TO HAPPEN WON'T BE SO BAD. . .
ARE YOU OKAY?
IT'S GONE NOW. BUT TH' GITCHY FEELIN' IS NEVER WRONG! YOU KEEP AN EYE ON THAT COUSIN OF YOURS, YOU HEAR?
YES MA'M!

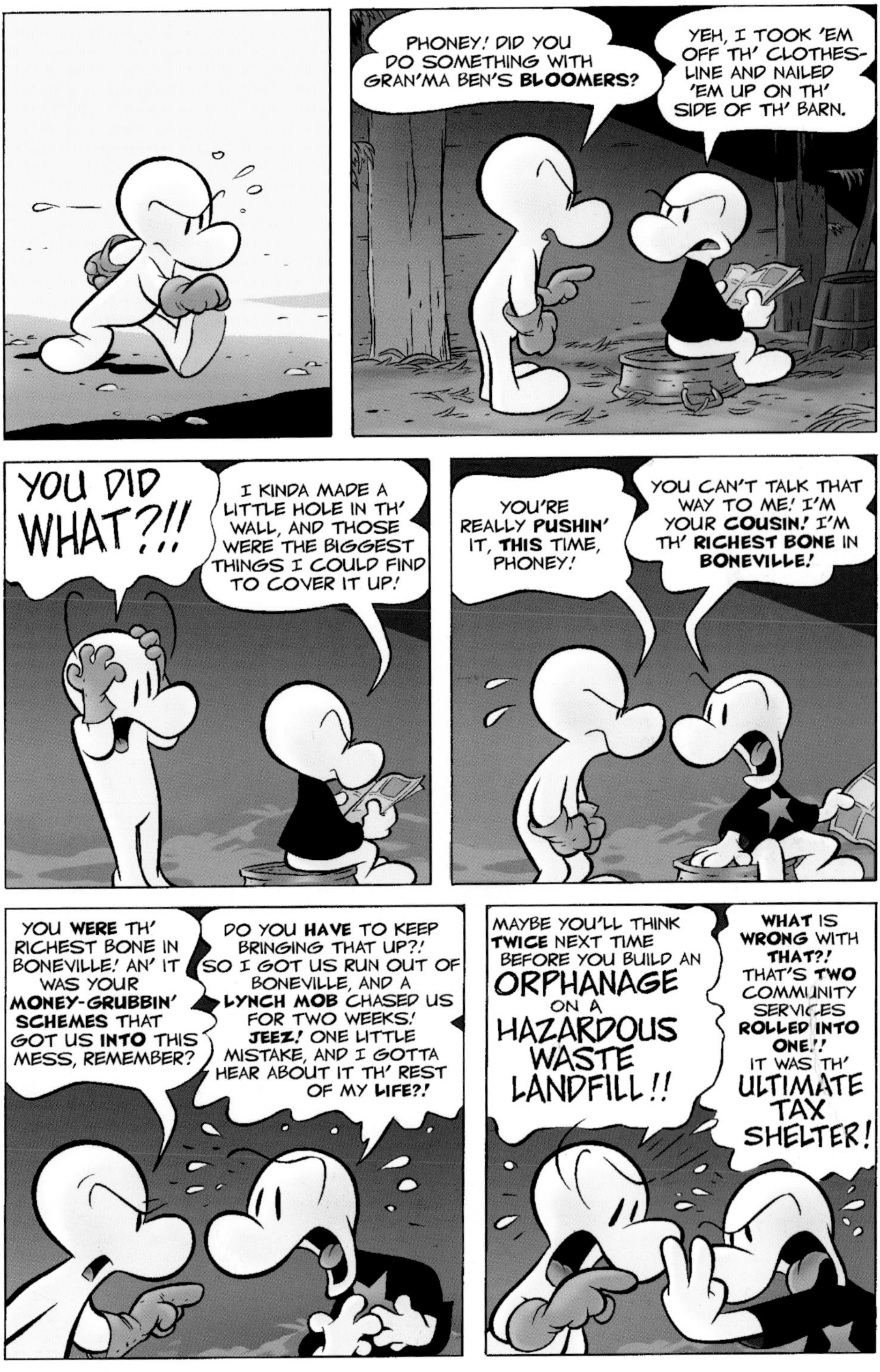
PHONEY! DID YOU DO SOMETHING WITH GRAN'MA BEN'S BLOOMERS?
YEH, I TOOK 'EM OFF TH' CLOTHES-LINE AND NAILED 'EM UP ON TH' SIDE OF TH' BARN.
YOU DID WHAT?!!
I KINDA MADE A LITTLE HOLE IN TH' WALL, AND THOSE WERE THE BIGGEST THINGS I COULD FIND TO COVER IT UP!
YOU'RE REALLY PUSHIN' IT, THIS TIME, PHONEY!
YOU CAN'T TALK THAT WAY TO ME! I'M YOUR COUSIN! I'M TH' RICHEST BONE IN BONEVILLE!
YOU WERE TH' RICHEST BONE IN BONEVILLE! AN' IT WAS YOUR MONEY-GRUBBIN' SCHEMES THAT GOT US INTO THIS MESS, REMEMBER?
DO YOU HAVE TO KEEP BRINGING THAT UP?! SO I GOT US RUN OUT OF BONEVILLE, AND A LYNCH MOB CHASED US FOR TWO WEEKS! JEEZ! ONE LITTLE MISTAKE, AND I GOTTA HEAR ABOUT IT TH' REST OF MY LIFE?!
MAYBE YOU'LL THINK TWICE NEXT TIME BEFORE YOU BUILD AN ORPHANAGE ON A HAZARDOUS WASTE LANDFILL!!
WHAT IS WRONG WITH THAT?! THAT'S TWO COMMUNITY SERVICES ROLLED INTO ONE!! IT WAS TH' ULTIMATE TAX SHELTER!

YOU **NEVER** LEARN, DO YOU?

I **SHOULDA** STUCK WITH MY FIRST IDEA!

WHAT? COMBINING A **SLAUGHTERHOUSE** WITH A **PETTING ZOO?!** OH, YEAH! **THAT** WAS **BRILLIANT!**

AHH! WHAT DO **YOU** KNOW?

CAN'T YOU MAKE IT THROUGH **ONE MORE DAY** WITHOUT GETTING US IN **TROUBLE?** WE'RE GOIN' INTO TOWN WITH GRAN'MA **TOMORROW!**

WHAT ARE WE WAITIN' FOR **HER** FOR? LET'S BLOW THIS POPSICLE STAND **NOW!**

TOMORROW IS TH' FIRST DAY OF TH' **SPRING FAIR!** THIS'LL BE OUR **BEST SHOT** AT FINDING SMILEY BONE!

GRAN'MA SAID THAT **LAST** WEEK PEOPLE WERE ALREADY COMIN' IN FROM **ALL OVER** TH' VALLEY- - - SETTIN' UP **BOOTHS** AN' GETTIN' **READY!**

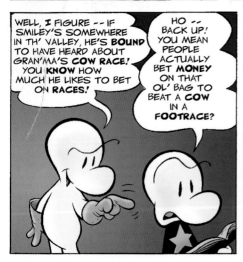

WELL, **I** FIGURE -- IF SMILEY'S SOMEWHERE IN TH' VALLEY, HE'S **BOUND** TO HAVE HEARD ABOUT GRAN'MA'S **COW RACE!** YOU **KNOW** HOW MUCH HE LIKES TO BET ON **RACES!**

HO -- BACK UP! YOU MEAN PEOPLE ACTUALLY BET **MONEY** ON THAT OL' BAG TO BEAT A **COW** IN A **FOOTRACE?**

I **KNOW!** IT'S **CRAZY**, BUT THORN SAYS IT'S A BIG **DEAL** HERE! SOME FOLKS BET EVERYTHING THEY'VE **GOT!**

OKAY, FONE BONE! **I'LL BE GOOD!** I POSITIVELY **GUARANTEE** YOU WON'T HEAR ANOTHER **PEEP** OUTTA ME ALL DAY!

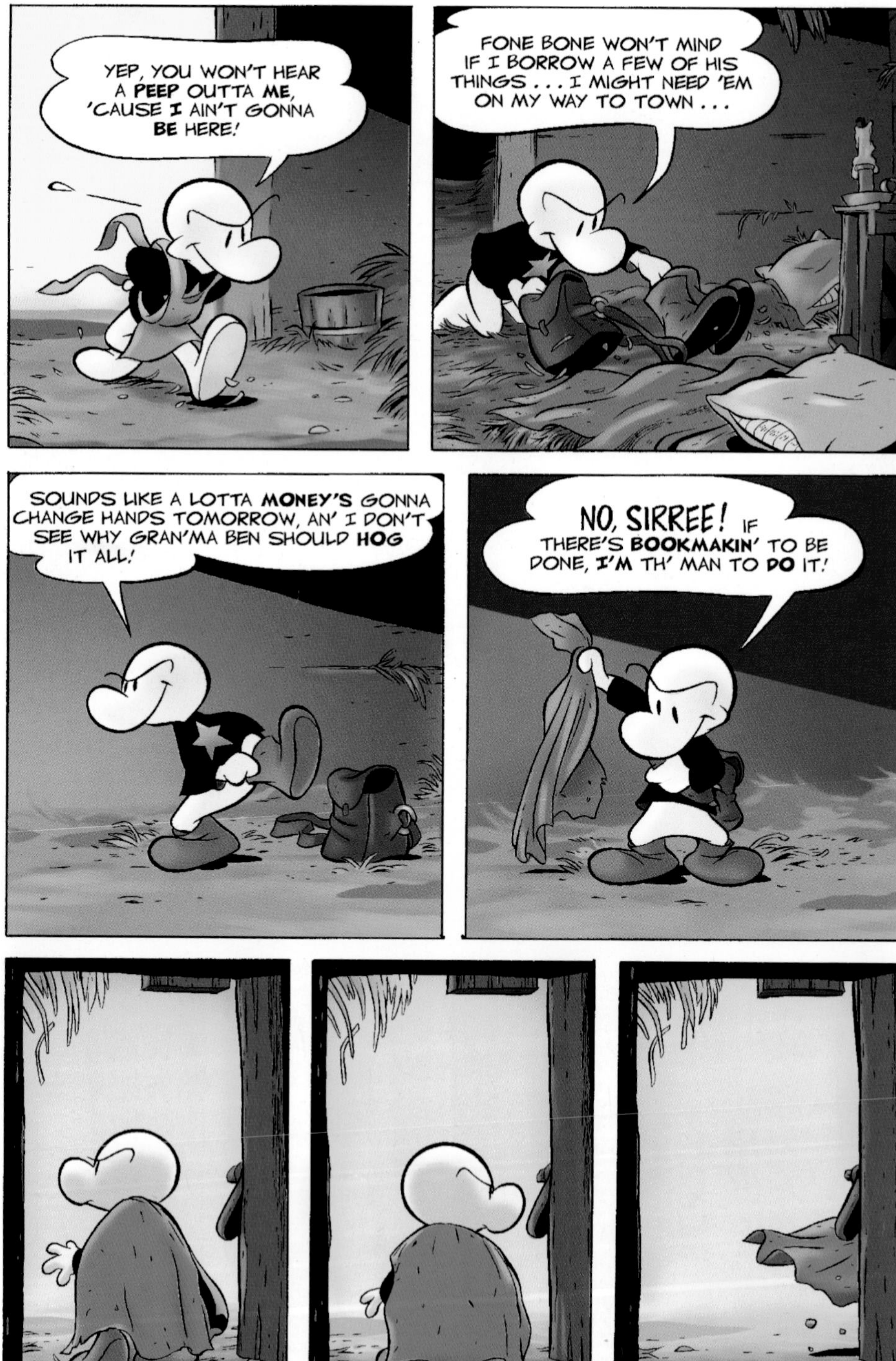
YEP, YOU WON'T HEAR A PEEP OUTTA ME, 'CAUSE I AIN'T GONNA BE HERE!
FONE BONE WON'T MIND IF I BORROW A FEW OF HIS THINGS . . . I MIGHT NEED 'EM ON MY WAY TO TOWN . . .
SOUNDS LIKE A LOTTA MONEY'S GONNA CHANGE HANDS TOMORROW, AN' I DON'T SEE WHY GRAN'MA BEN SHOULD HOG IT ALL!
NO, SIRREE! IF THERE'S BOOKMAKIN' TO BE DONE, I'M TH' MAN TO DO IT!

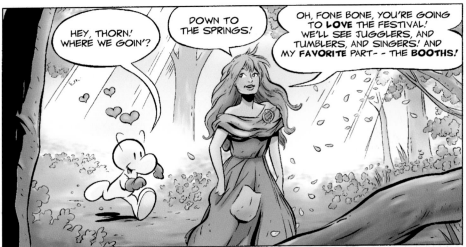

HEY, THORN! WHERE WE GOIN'?

DOWN TO THE SPRINGS!

OH, FONE BONE, YOU'RE GOING TO **LOVE** THE FESTIVAL! WE'LL SEE JUGGLERS, AND TUMBLERS, AND SINGERS! AND MY **FAVORITE** PART-- THE **BOOTHS!**

THERE ARE **ROWS** AND **ROWS** OF **BOOTHS**, AND YOU CAN BUY THE MOST **AMAZING** THINGS! THEY HAVE **HONEY**, AND **PEACOCK FEATHERS**, AND **SILK ROBES!**

I USUALLY ONLY GET TO LOOK-- BUT **THIS** YEAR I'M GOING TO GET A BOTTLE OF **DYE** FROM THE SOUTH, AND I'M GOING TO MAKE A BEAUTIFUL **BLUE DRESS!**

HOW COME WE DIDN'T BRING ANY BUCKETS TO CARRY TH' WATER BACK IN?

WE'RE NOT GETTING WATER.

WE'RE TAKING A BATH!

A BATH? WHAT **KIND** OF BATH?

OHMYGOSH

YOU WANT TO GET CLEANED UP FOR THE FESTIVAL, DON'T YOU? C'MON!

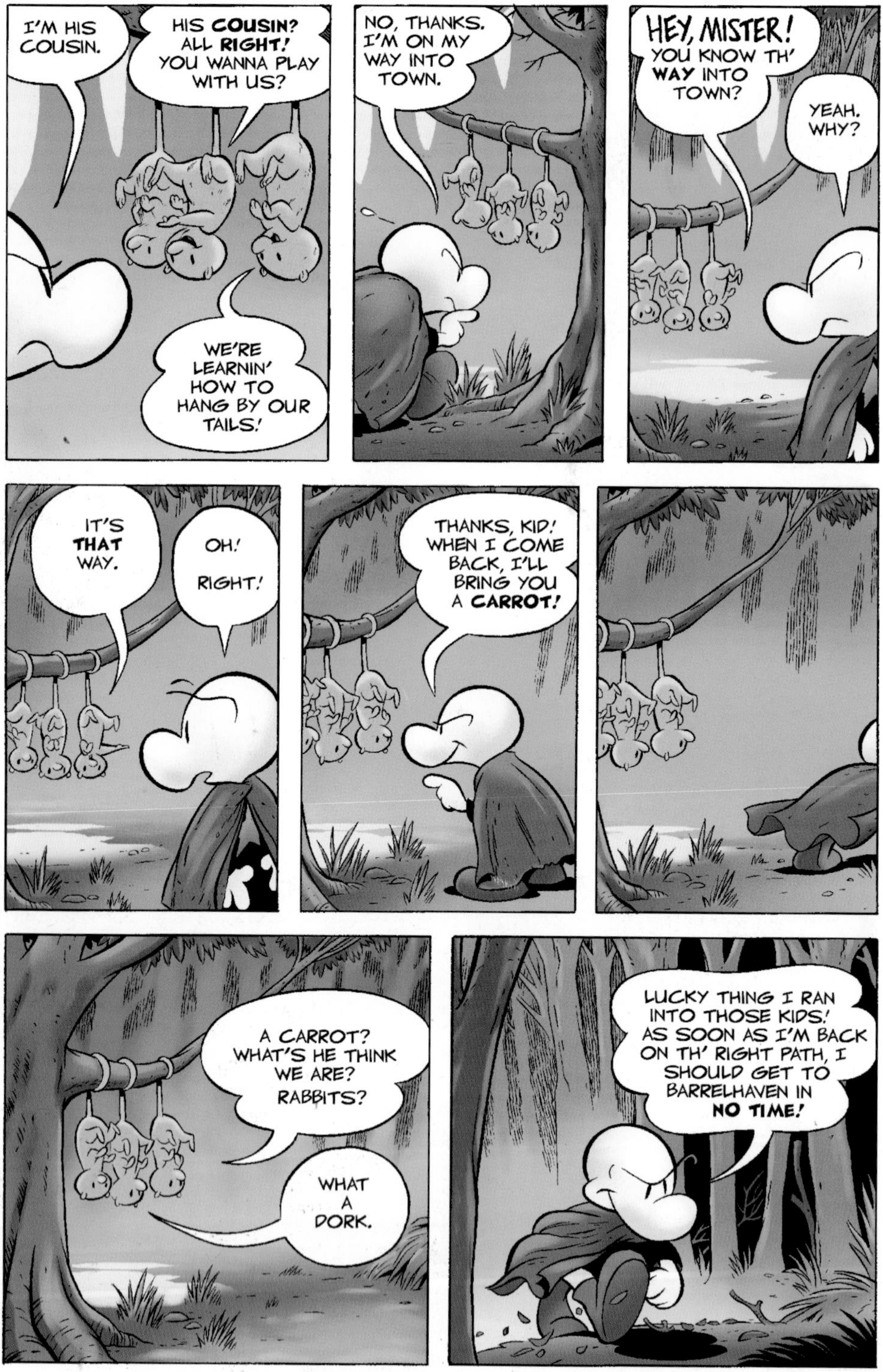
I'M HIS COUSIN.
HIS COUSIN? ALL RIGHT! YOU WANNA PLAY WITH US?
WE'RE LEARNIN' HOW TO HANG BY OUR TAILS!
NO, THANKS. I'M ON MY WAY INTO TOWN.
HEY, MISTER! YOU KNOW TH' WAY INTO TOWN?
YEAH. WHY?
IT'S THAT WAY.
OH! RIGHT!
THANKS, KID! WHEN I COME BACK, I'LL BRING YOU A CARROT!
A CARROT? WHAT'S HE THINK WE ARE? RABBITS?
WHAT A DORK.
LUCKY THING I RAN INTO THOSE KIDS! AS SOON AS I'M BACK ON TH' RIGHT PATH, I SHOULD GET TO BARRELHAVEN IN NO TIME!

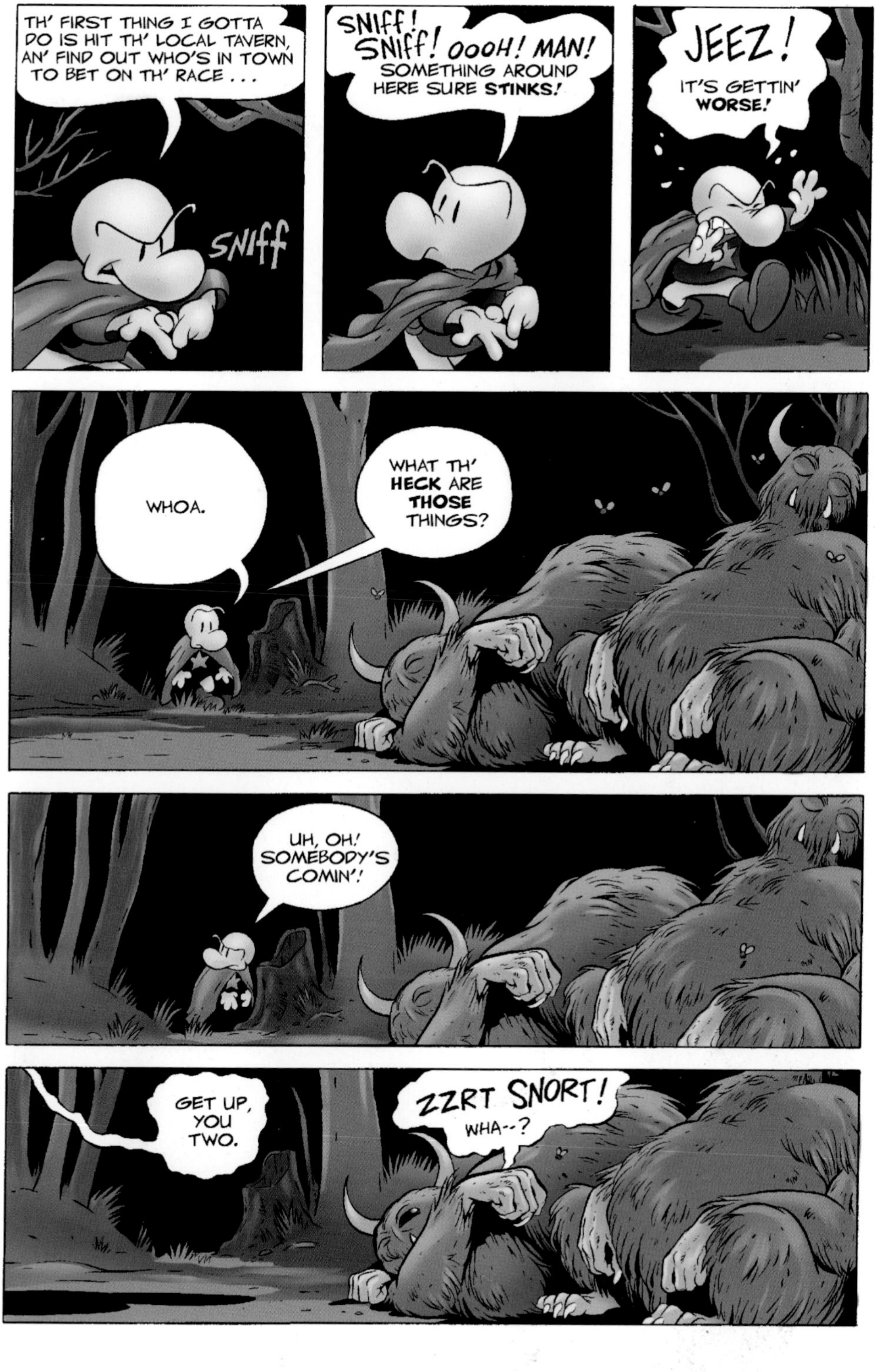
TH' FIRST THING I GOTTA DO IS HIT TH' LOCAL TAVERN, AN' FIND OUT WHO'S IN TOWN TO BET ON TH' RACE . . .
SNIFF
SNIFF! SNIFF! OOOH! MAN! SOMETHING AROUND HERE SURE STINKS!
JEEZ! IT'S GETTIN' WORSE!
WHOA.
WHAT TH' HECK ARE THOSE THINGS?
UH, OH! SOMEBODY'S COMIN'!
GET UP, YOU TWO.
ZZRT SNORT! WHA--?

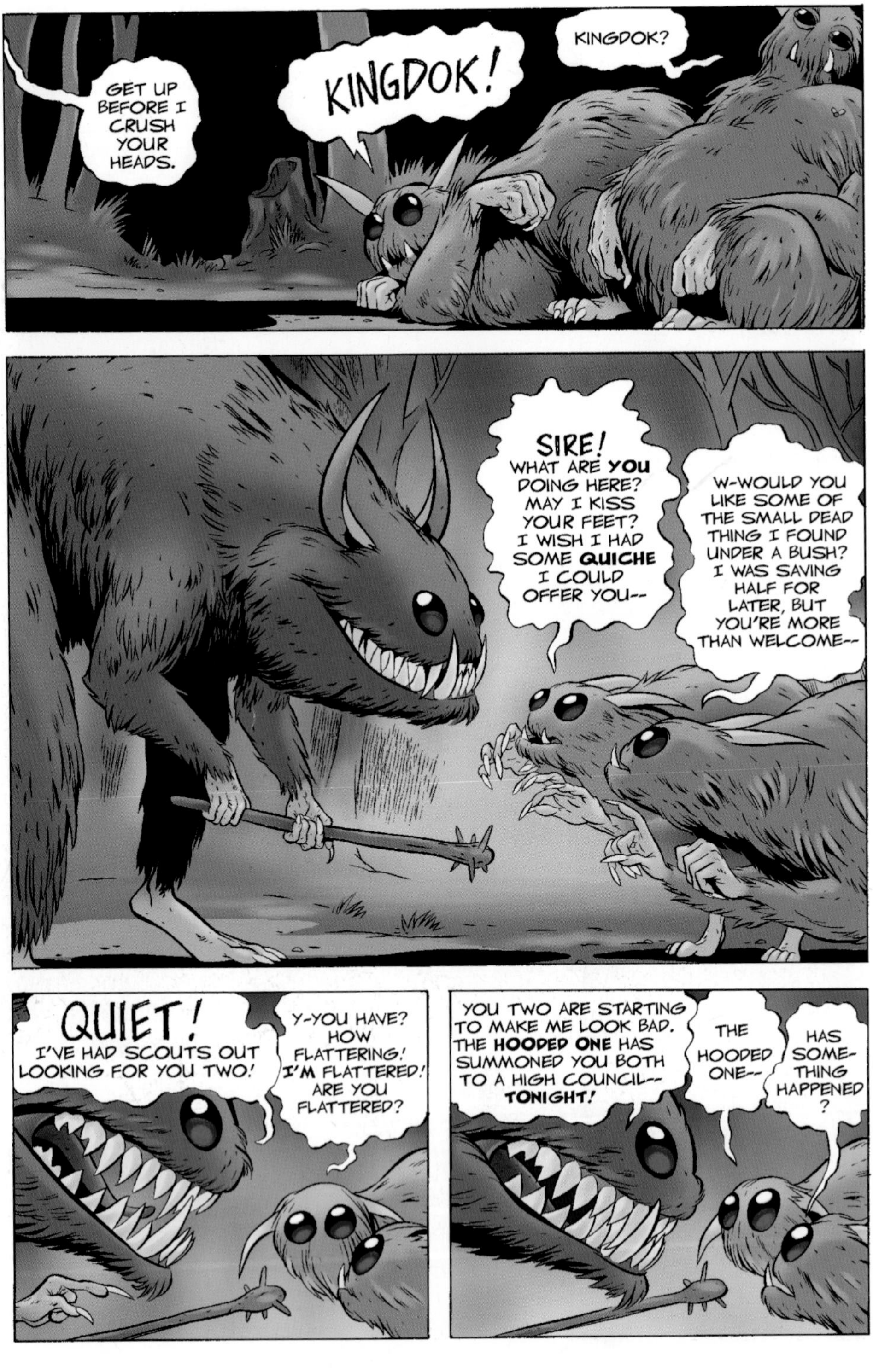
GET UP BEFORE I CRUSH YOUR HEADS.
KINGDOK!
KINGDOK?
SIRE! WHAT ARE YOU DOING HERE? MAY I KISS YOUR FEET? I WISH I HAD SOME QUICHE I COULD OFFER YOU--
W-WOULD YOU LIKE SOME OF THE SMALL DEAD THING I FOUND UNDER A BUSH? I WAS SAVING HALF FOR LATER, BUT YOU'RE MORE THAN WELCOME--
QUIET! I'VE HAD SCOUTS OUT LOOKING FOR YOU TWO!
Y-YOU HAVE? HOW FLATTERING! I'M FLATTERED! ARE YOU FLATTERED?
YOU TWO ARE STARTING TO MAKE ME LOOK BAD. THE HOODED ONE HAS SUMMONED YOU BOTH TO A HIGH COUNCIL-- TONIGHT!
THE HOODED ONE--
HAS SOMETHING HAPPENED?

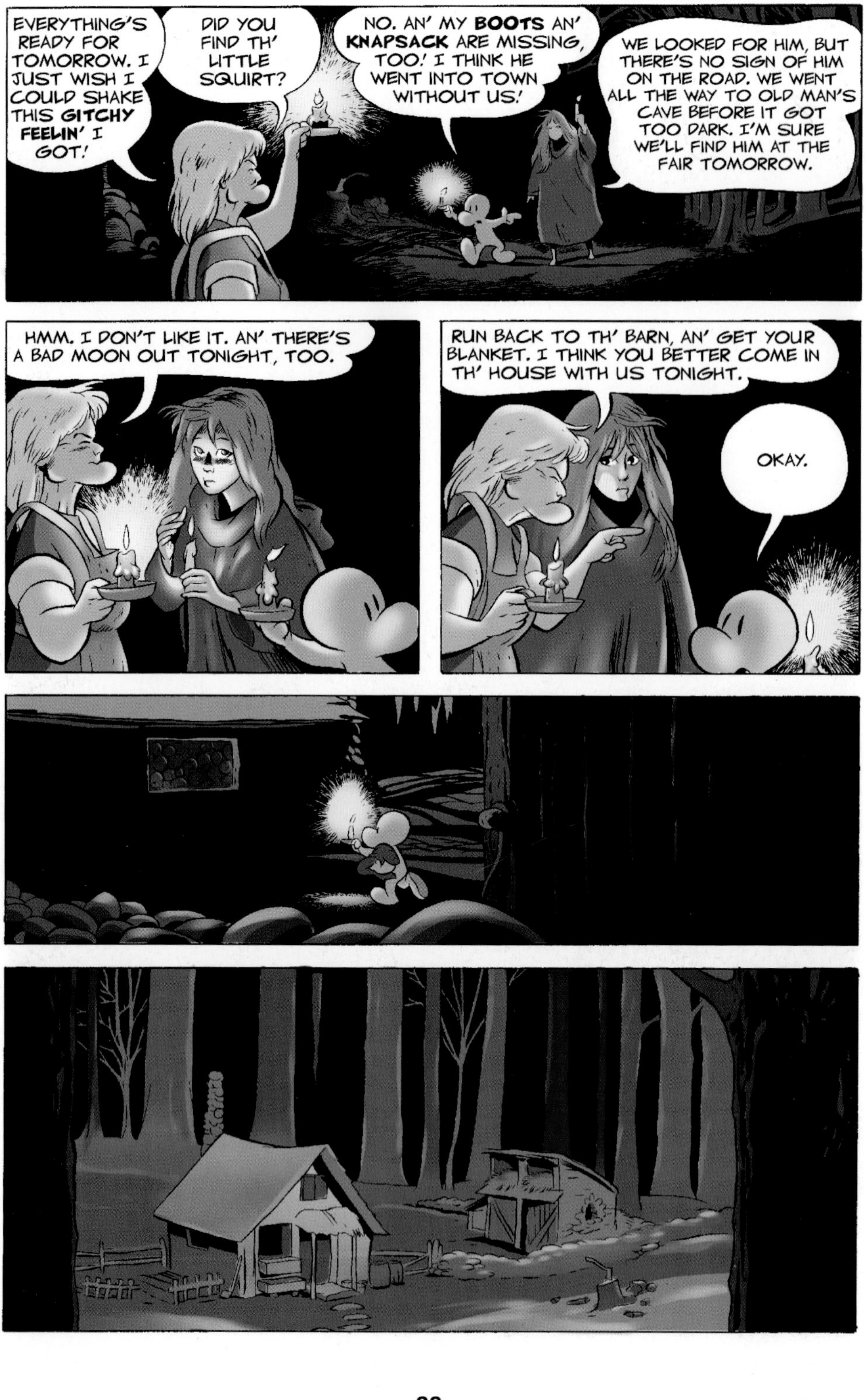
EVERYTHING'S READY FOR TOMORROW. I JUST WISH I COULD SHAKE THIS **GITCHY FEELIN'** I GOT!
DID YOU FIND TH' LITTLE SQUIRT?
NO. AN' MY **BOOTS** AN' **KNAPSACK** ARE MISSING, TOO! I THINK HE WENT INTO TOWN WITHOUT US!
WE LOOKED FOR HIM, BUT THERE'S NO SIGN OF HIM ON THE ROAD. WE WENT ALL THE WAY TO OLD MAN'S CAVE BEFORE IT GOT TOO DARK. I'M SURE WE'LL FIND HIM AT THE FAIR TOMORROW.
HMM. I DON'T LIKE IT. AN' THERE'S A BAD MOON OUT TONIGHT, TOO.
RUN BACK TO TH' BARN, AN' GET YOUR BLANKET. I THINK YOU BETTER COME IN TH' HOUSE WITH US TONIGHT.
OKAY.

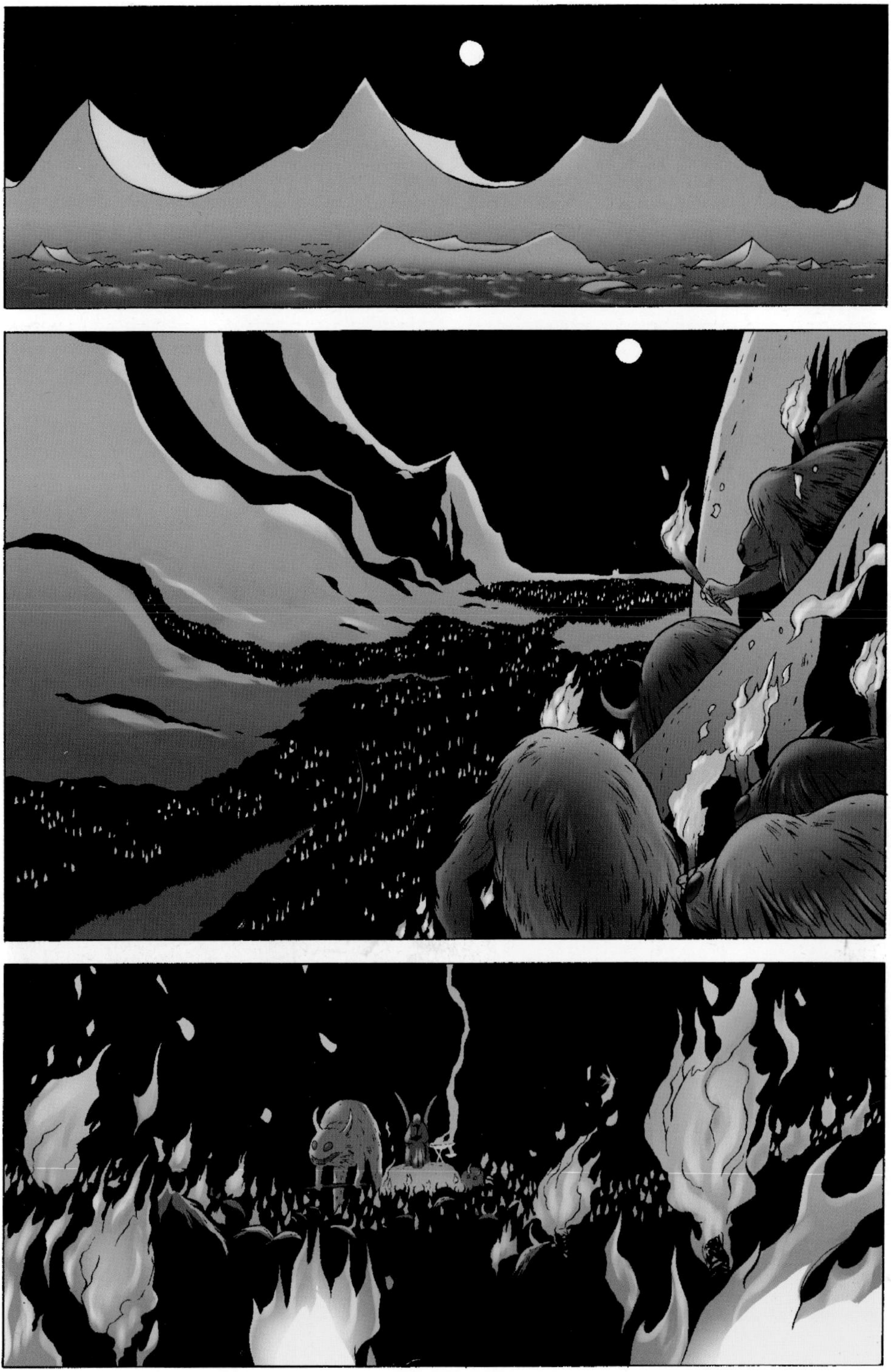

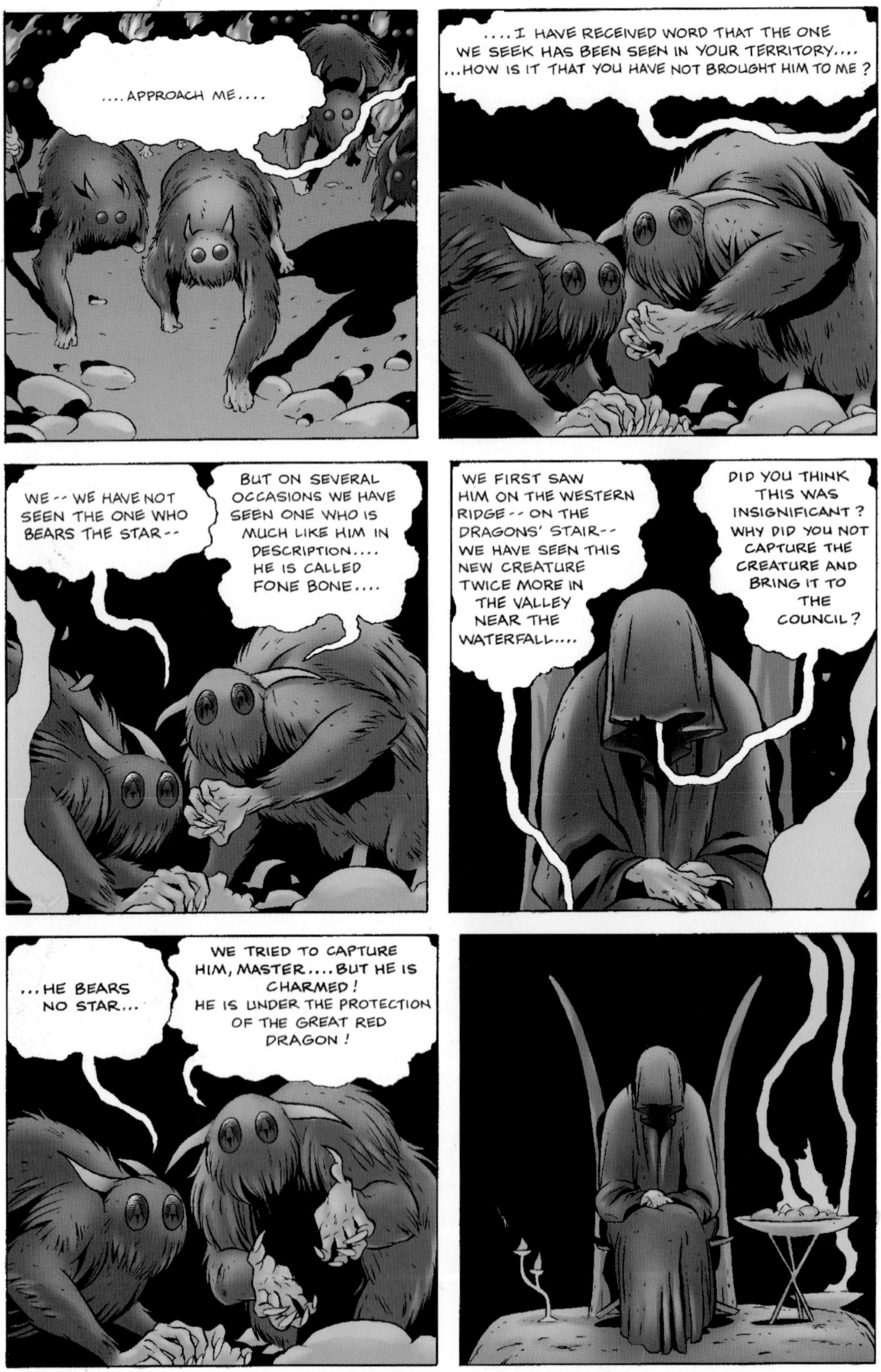
....APPROACH ME....
....I HAVE RECEIVED WORD THAT THE ONE WE SEEK HAS BEEN SEEN IN YOUR TERRITORY.... ...HOW IS IT THAT YOU HAVE NOT BROUGHT HIM TO ME ?
WE -- WE HAVE NOT SEEN THE ONE WHO BEARS THE STAR --
BUT ON SEVERAL OCCASIONS WE HAVE SEEN ONE WHO IS MUCH LIKE HIM IN DESCRIPTION.... HE IS CALLED FONE BONE....
WE FIRST SAW HIM ON THE WESTERN RIDGE -- ON THE DRAGONS' STAIR -- WE HAVE SEEN THIS NEW CREATURE TWICE MORE IN THE VALLEY NEAR THE WATERFALL....
DID YOU THINK THIS WAS INSIGNIFICANT ? WHY DID YOU NOT CAPTURE THE CREATURE AND BRING IT TO THE COUNCIL ?
...HE BEARS NO STAR...
WE TRIED TO CAPTURE HIM, MASTER.... BUT HE IS CHARMED ! HE IS UNDER THE PROTECTION OF THE GREAT RED DRAGON !

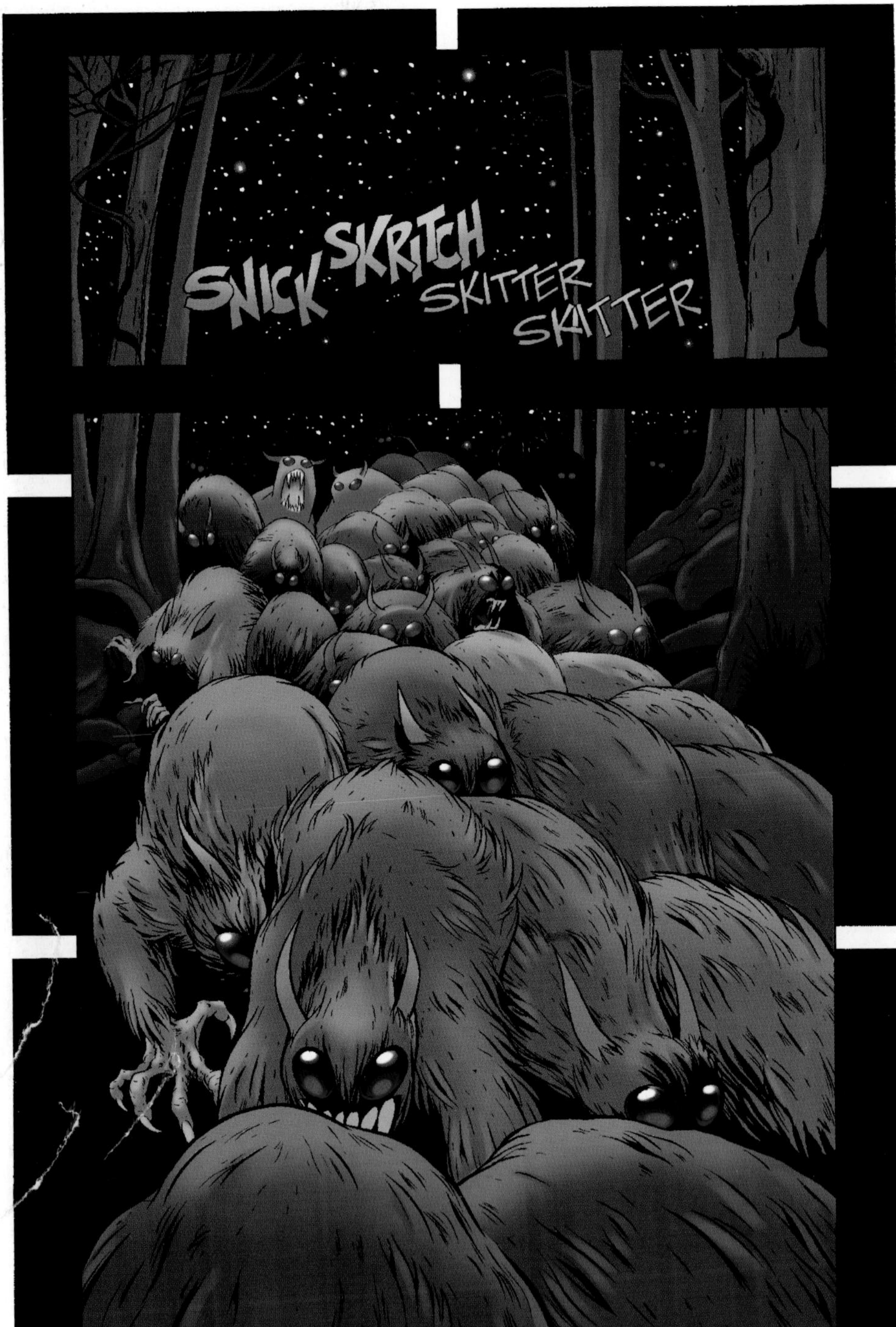
SNICK
SKRITCH
SKITTER
SKITTER

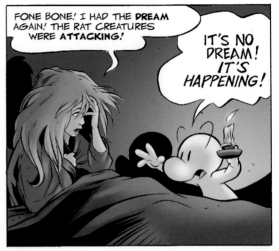

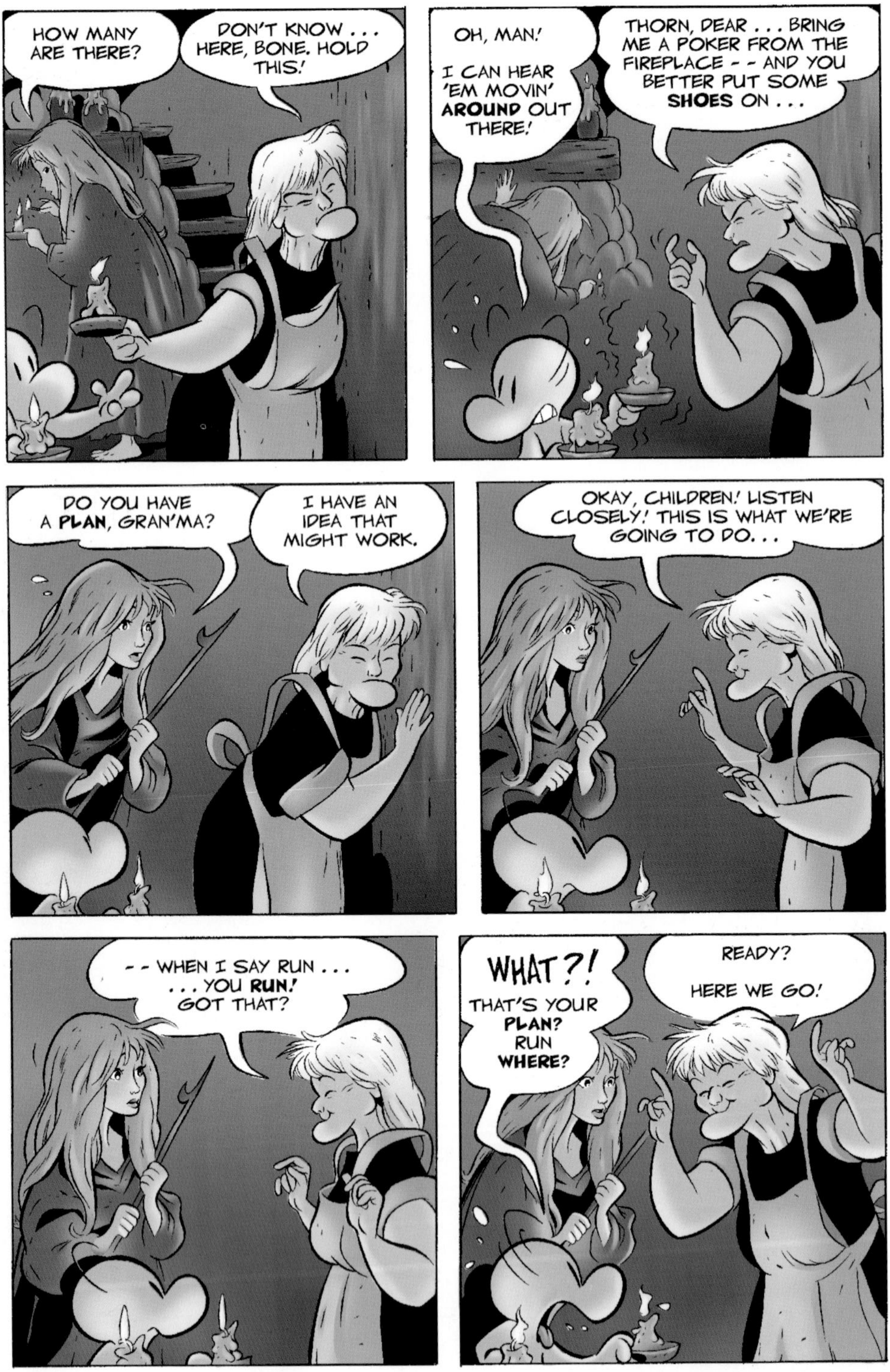
HOW MANY ARE THERE?
DON'T KNOW . . . HERE, BONE. HOLD THIS!
OH, MAN!
I CAN HEAR 'EM MOVIN' AROUND OUT THERE!
THORN, DEAR . . . BRING ME A POKER FROM THE FIREPLACE - - AND YOU BETTER PUT SOME SHOES ON . . .
DO YOU HAVE A PLAN, GRAN'MA?
I HAVE AN IDEA THAT MIGHT WORK.
OKAY, CHILDREN! LISTEN CLOSELY! THIS IS WHAT WE'RE GOING TO DO. . .
- - WHEN I SAY RUN . . . . . . YOU RUN! GOT THAT?
WHAT?!
THAT'S YOUR PLAN? RUN WHERE?
READY?
HERE WE GO!

CRASSSH
SPLINTER

K-K-R-R-K

OKAY, KIDS! RUN!

CRUNCH

UH . . .

NOW, BONE!

WE CAN'T JUST **LEAVE** YOU HERE!

COME **ON**, FONE BONE!

DON'T WORRY ABOUT **ME**--

B!F!

SPLAT!

I FOUGHT TH' RATS BACK IN TH' **BIG** WAR!

OHMYGOSH

THUD THUD! WAK!

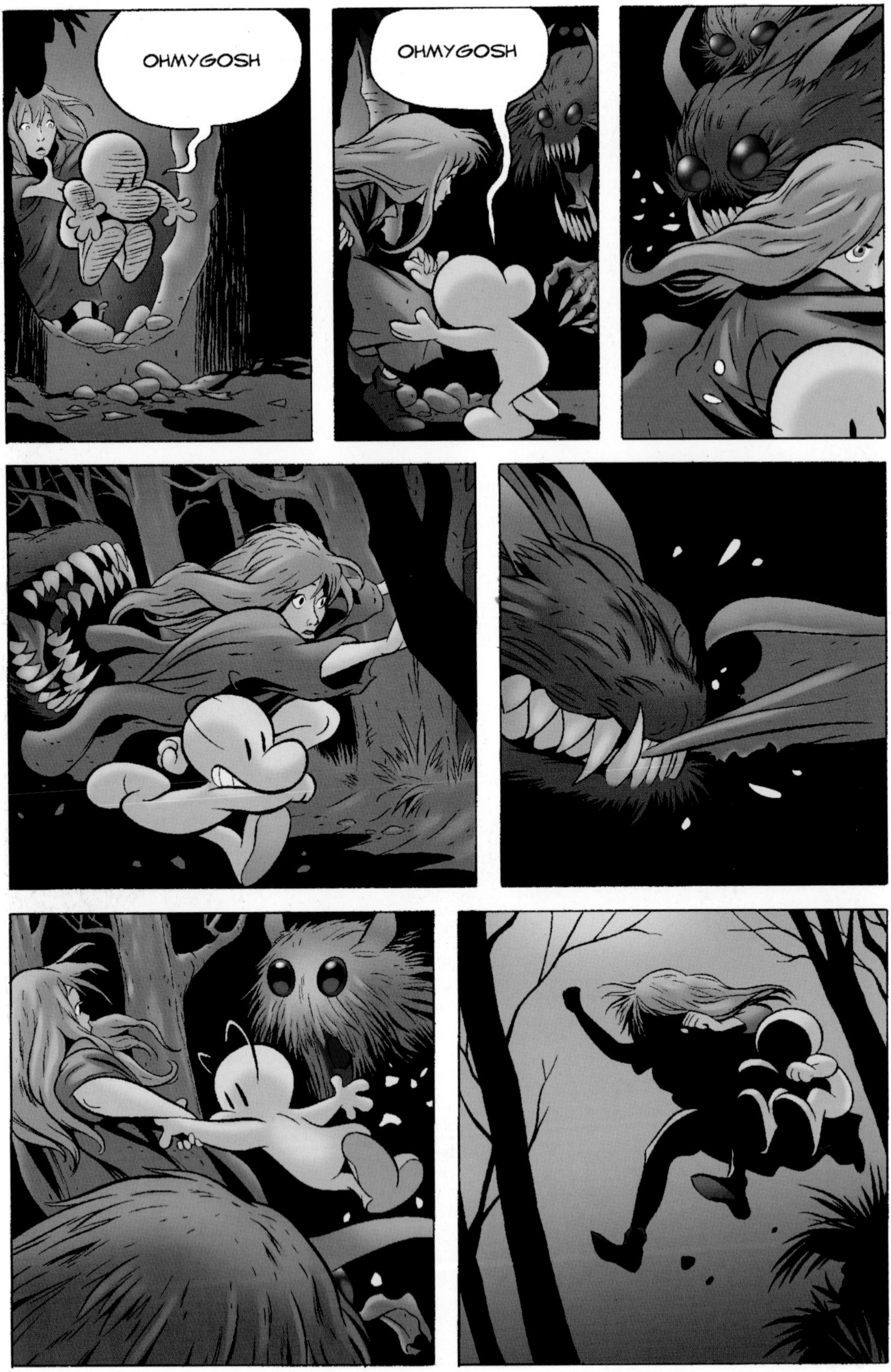
OHMYGOSH
OHMYGOSH

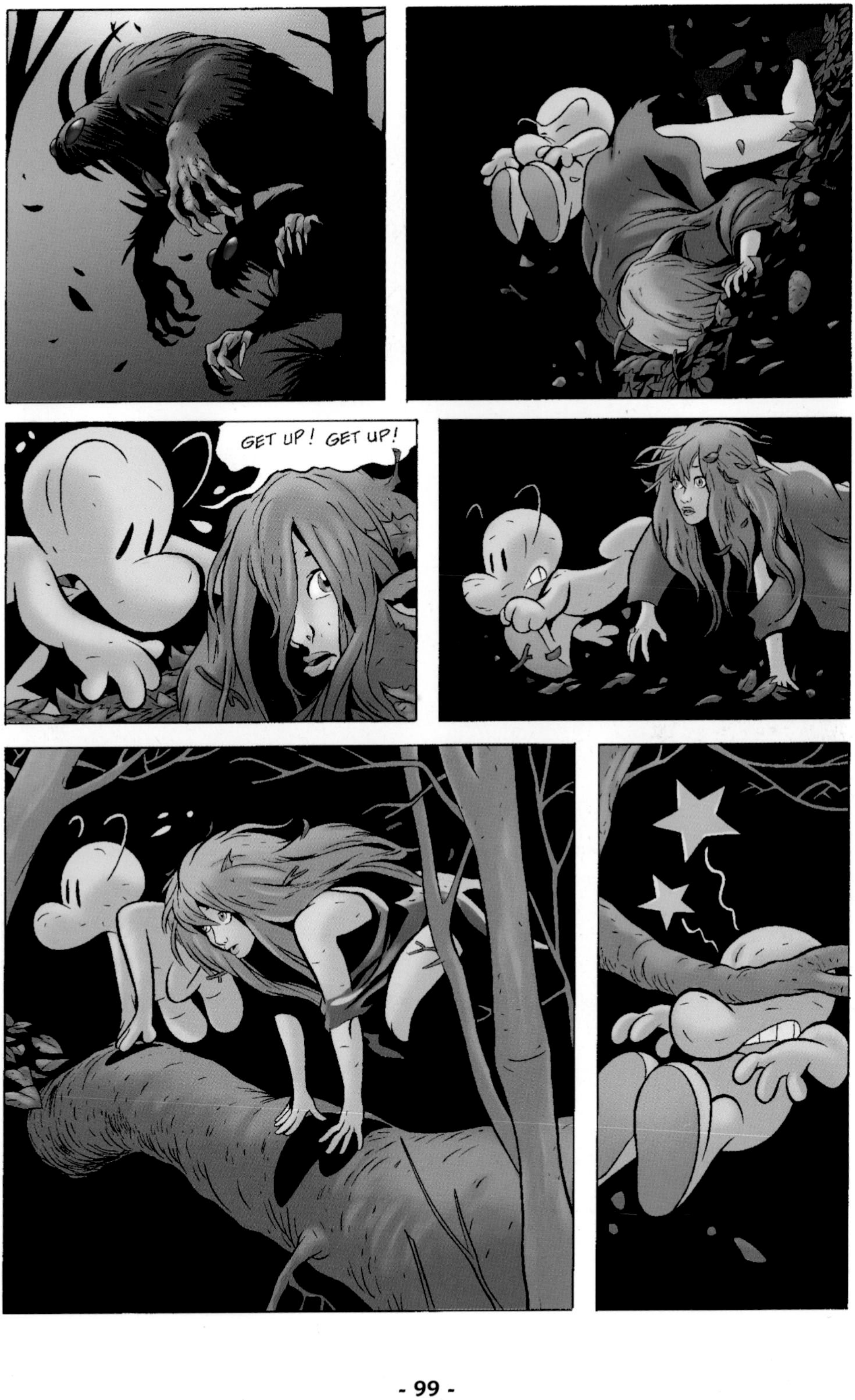
GET UP! GET UP!

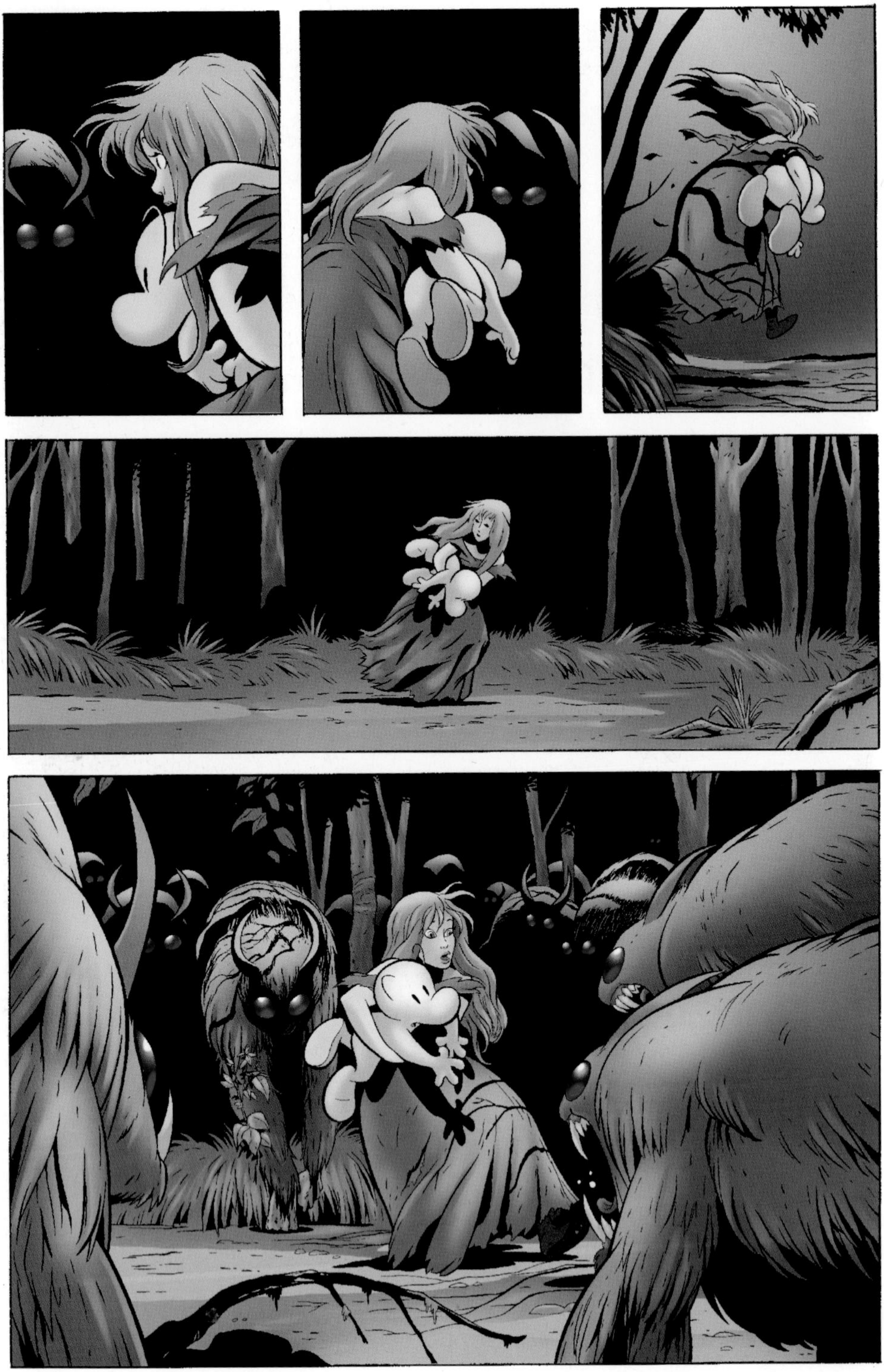

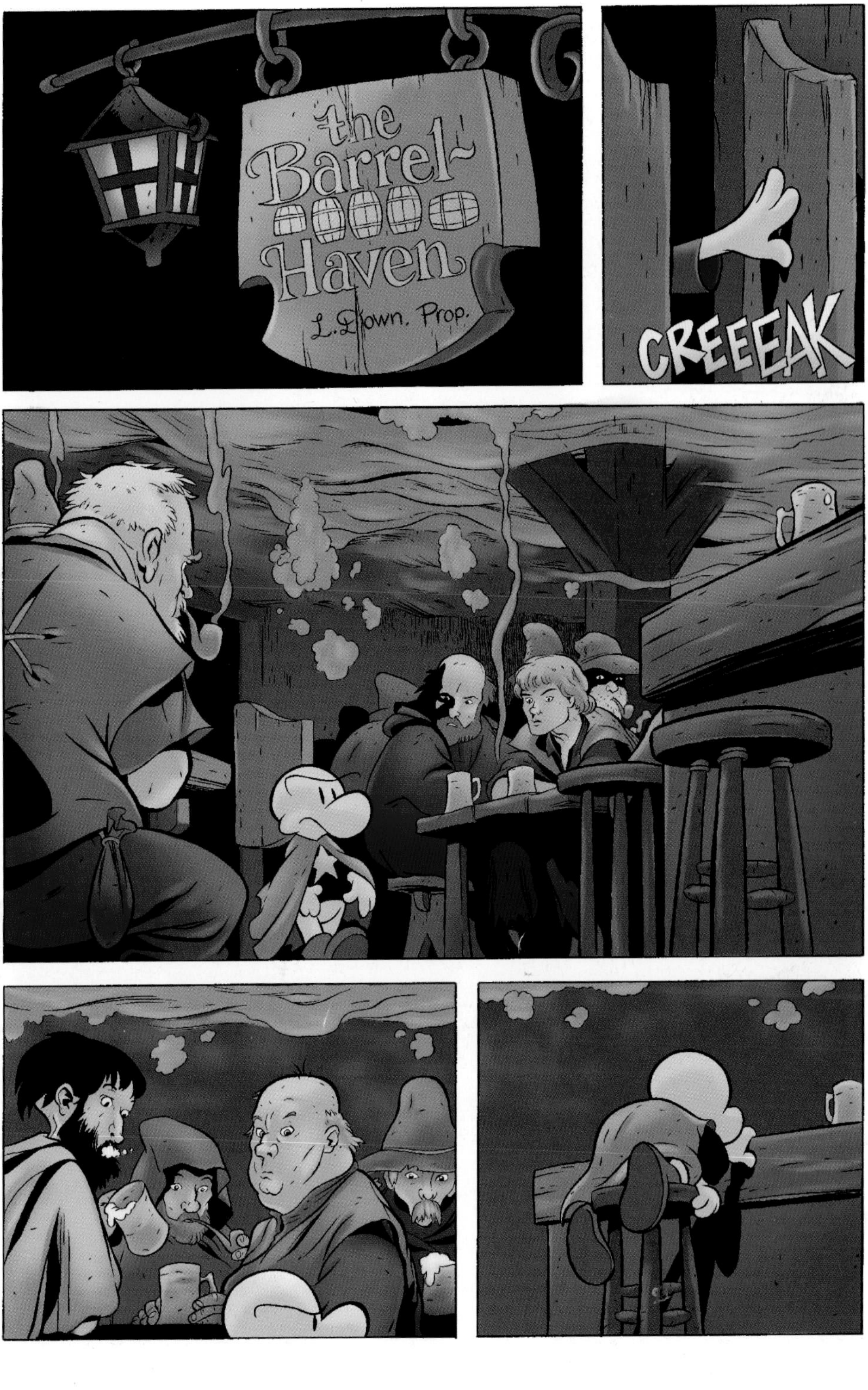
the Barrel~
Haven
L. Down. Prop.
CREEEAK

IT **IS** YOU! THANK **GOODNESS** I'VE **FOUND** YOU!!

YA **MEAN** IT, PHONEY? YOU'RE **HAPPY** TO SEE ME?

DARN RIGHT!! FONE BONE WOULDN'T LET ME **LEAVE** THIS STUPID VALLEY UNLESS I **FOUND** YOU FIRST!

AW, SHUCKS -- IT'S GOOD TO SEE YOU, **TOO**, CUZ!

THIS CALLS FOR A **TOAST!** LET ME BUY YOU A **DRINK**, OL' **BUDDY!**

OKAY BY **ME**, OL' **PAL!**

HERE'S TO GOIN' **HOME!**

TO BONEVILLE!

CLINK

TO BONEVILLE!

GLUG! GLUG!

AHH!

SMEK SMEK

WHADDYA SAY WE HAVE ANOTHER ROUND ON **YOU**, OL' **FRIEND!**

SURE! WHY **NOT?** I GOT A FEELIN' MY **LUCK'S** ABOUT TO **CHANGE!** -- **GUESS** WHERE FONE BONE IS **RIGHT NOW!** HE'S WITH **GRAN'MA BEN!** YOU KNOW - - TH' OLD LADY THAT RACES **COWS!**

AH! YOU'RE IN TOWN FOR TH' **COW RACE!** ME TOO! THERE'S GONNA BE SOME HEAVY **BETTIN'** GOIN' ON!

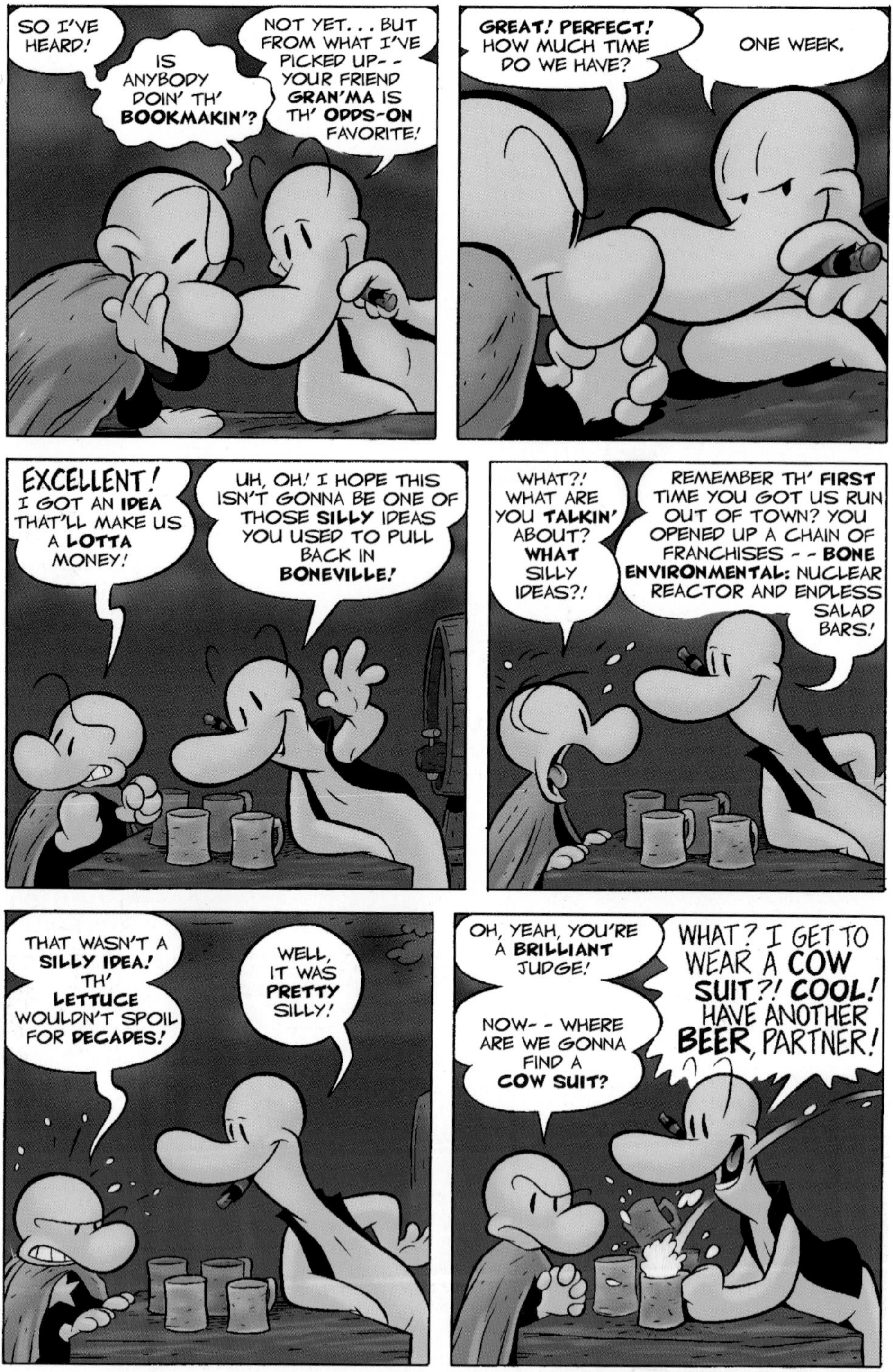
SO I'VE HEARD!
IS ANYBODY DOIN' TH' BOOKMAKIN'?
NOT YET. . . BUT FROM WHAT I'VE PICKED UP- - YOUR FRIEND GRAN'MA IS TH' ODDS-ON FAVORITE!
GREAT! PERFECT! HOW MUCH TIME DO WE HAVE?
ONE WEEK.
EXCELLENT! I GOT AN IDEA THAT'LL MAKE US A LOTTA MONEY!
UH, OH! I HOPE THIS ISN'T GONNA BE ONE OF THOSE SILLY IDEAS YOU USED TO PULL BACK IN BONEVILLE!
WHAT?! WHAT ARE YOU TALKIN' ABOUT? WHAT SILLY IDEAS?!
REMEMBER TH' FIRST TIME YOU GOT US RUN OUT OF TOWN? YOU OPENED UP A CHAIN OF FRANCHISES - - BONE ENVIRONMENTAL: NUCLEAR REACTOR AND ENDLESS SALAD BARS!
THAT WASN'T A SILLY IDEA! TH' LETTUCE WOULDN'T SPOIL FOR DECADES!
WELL, IT WAS PRETTY SILLY!
OH, YEAH, YOU'RE A BRILLIANT JUDGE!
NOW- - WHERE ARE WE GONNA FIND A COW SUIT?
WHAT? I GET TO WEAR A COW SUIT?! COOL! HAVE ANOTHER BEER, PARTNER!

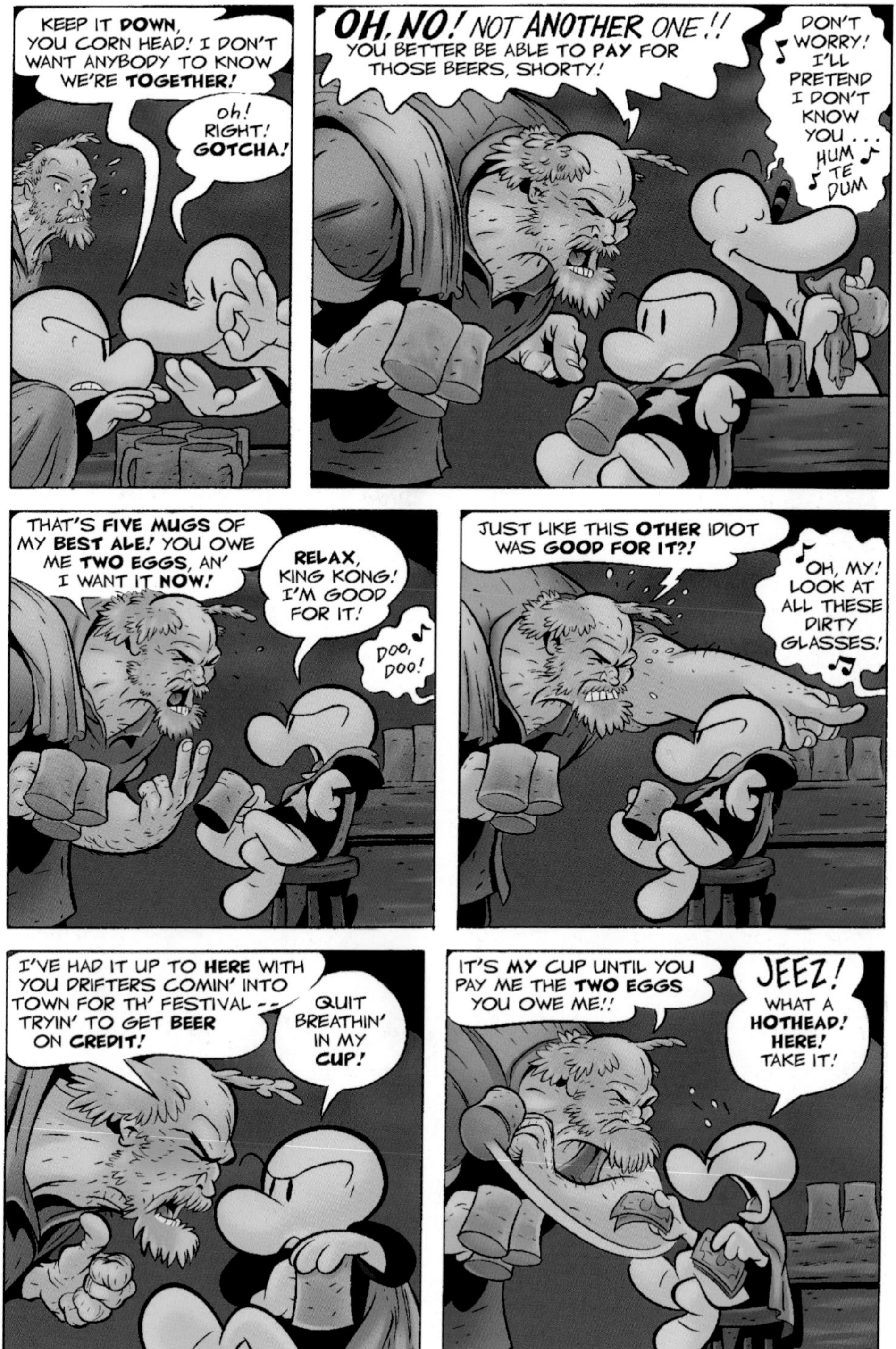
KEEP IT DOWN, YOU CORN HEAD! I DON'T WANT ANYBODY TO KNOW WE'RE TOGETHER!
oh! RIGHT! GOTCHA!
OH, NO! NOT ANOTHER ONE!! YOU BETTER BE ABLE TO PAY FOR THOSE BEERS, SHORTY!
DON'T WORRY! I'LL PRETEND I DON'T KNOW YOU... HUM TE DUM
THAT'S FIVE MUGS OF MY BEST ALE! YOU OWE ME TWO EGGS, AN' I WANT IT NOW!
RELAX, KING KONG! I'M GOOD FOR IT!
DOO, DOO!
JUST LIKE THIS OTHER IDIOT WAS GOOD FOR IT?!
OH, MY! LOOK AT ALL THESE DIRTY GLASSES!
I'VE HAD IT UP TO HERE WITH YOU DRIFTERS COMIN' INTO TOWN FOR TH' FESTIVAL -- TRYIN' TO GET BEER ON CREDIT!
QUIT BREATHIN' IN MY CUP!
IT'S MY CUP UNTIL YOU PAY ME THE TWO EGGS YOU OWE ME!!
JEEZ! WHAT A HOTHEAD! HERE! TAKE IT!

WHAT'S THIS?

TWO **EGGS**, PAL! WHAT? DID TH' PRICE GO UP?

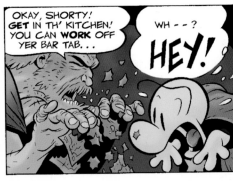

OKAY, SHORTY! **GET** IN TH' KITCHEN! YOU CAN **WORK** OFF YER BAR TAB...

WH--?

HEY!

NOBODY MUTILATES A **MINT NOTE** AROUND **ME** AN' LIVES TO **TELL** ABOUT IT! **SAY YER PRAYERS, CHUCKLES!**

THEY DON'T **USE** MONEY HERE, CUZ! THEY'VE NEVER EVEN **SEEN** IT BEFORE!

COME AGAIN?

THEY TRADE **GOODS** AND **SERVICES.** IT'S A **BARTER SYSTEM!**

CHUCKLES WANTS **REAL EGGS!**

YOUR BUTT IS **MINE,** BALDY!

SMILEY -- **WHY** DID YOU KEEP GIVING ME BEER? YOU **KNOW** I DON'T CARRY **DAIRY PRODUCTS !!**

UH, OH! LOOKS LIKE I MISSED SOME OF THOSE DIRTY GLASSES!

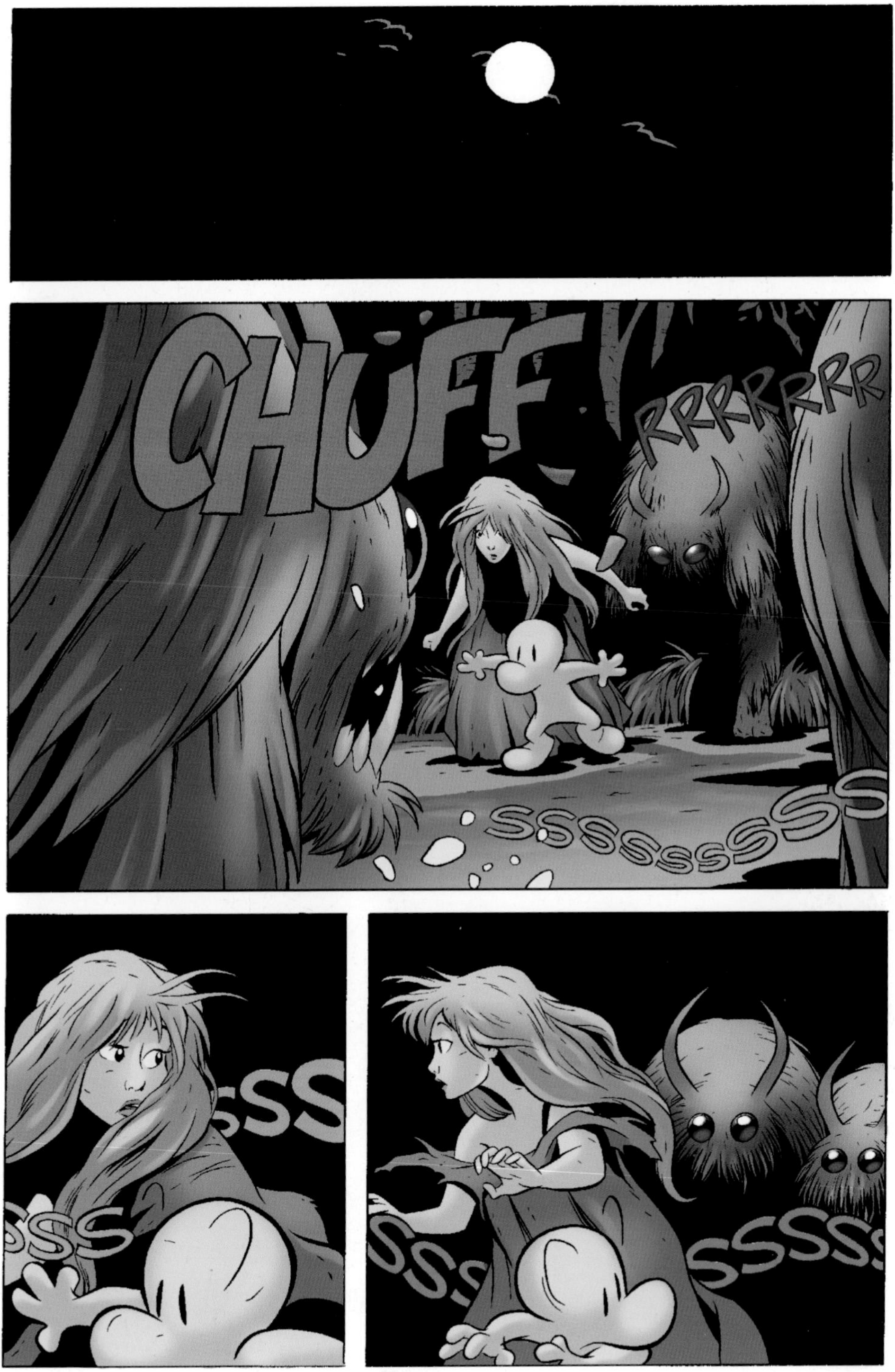
CHUFF
RRRRRRR
SSSSSSSSSS
SSS
SSS
SSS
SSSSS

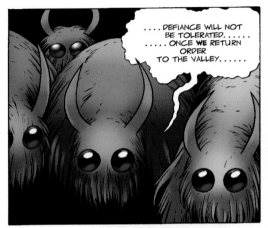

.... DEFIANCE WILL NOT BE TOLERATED...... ..... ONCE **WE** RETURN ORDER TO THE VALLEY......

STAY BACK!

SNIFF! SNIFF!

WAIT A MINUTE! WAIT A MINUTE!

DO YOU **SMELL** THAT?!

IT'S BRIMSTONE! IT'S THE DRAGON! HE'S HERE!

OH, NO.

RELAX, THORN! EVERYTHING'S GONNA BE **OKAY!**

FONE BONE! WHAT ARE YOU DOING?!

I KNOW **YOU** DON'T BELIEVE IN DRAGONS, BUT **THESE** GUYS DO! WATCH **THIS!**

HE **DID** IT! **YES!** I **TOLD** YOU THERE WAS A DRAGON! I **TOLD** YOU!

MR. DRAGON...

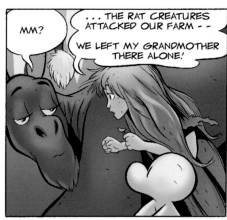

MM?

... THE RAT CREATURES ATTACKED OUR FARM --

WE LEFT MY GRANDMOTHER THERE ALONE!

CLIMB ON MY BACK.

C'MON, FONE BONE!

OHMYGOSH

HOLD TIGHT!

HURRY!

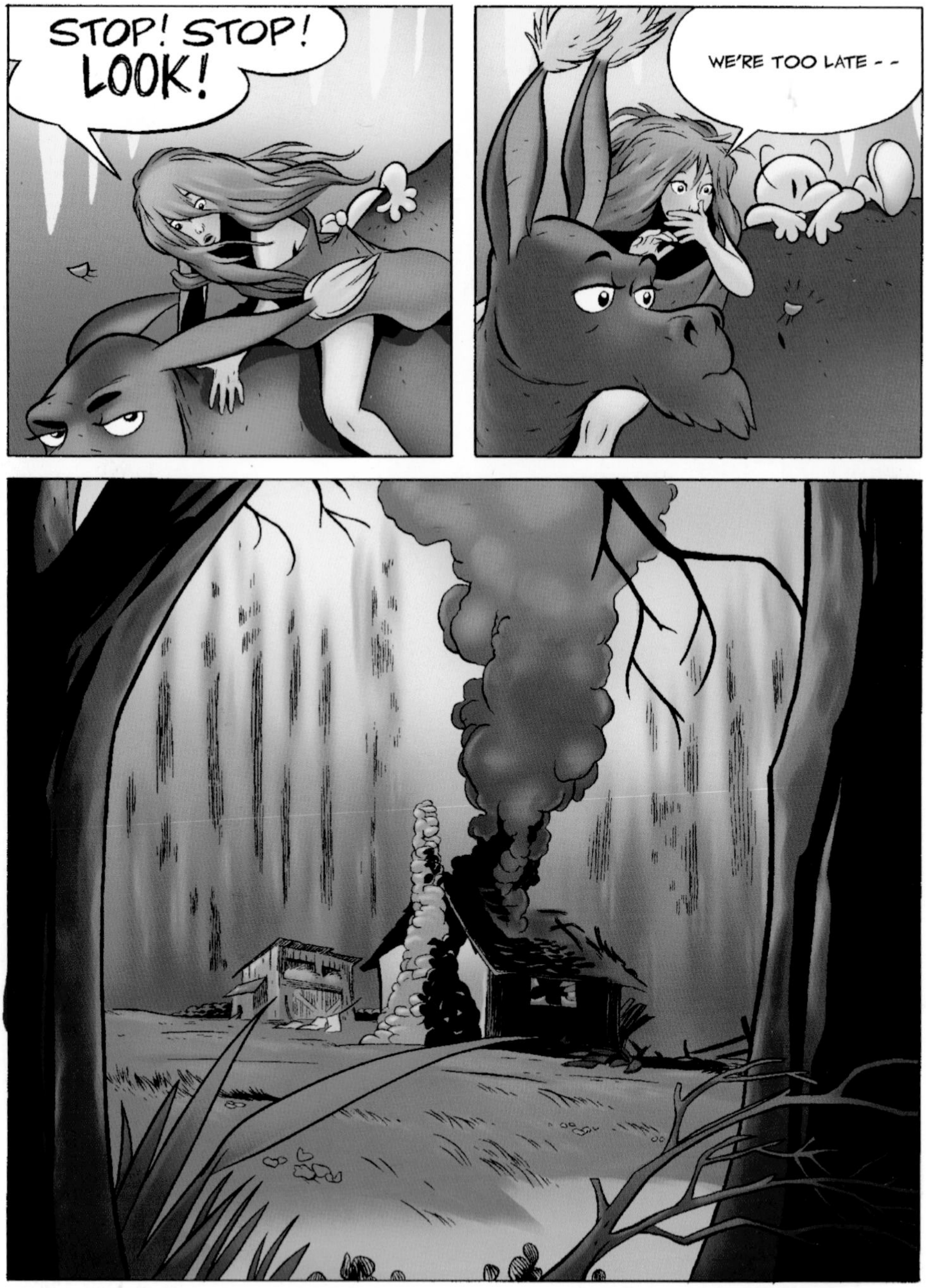
STOP! STOP! LOOK!
WE'RE TOO LATE - -

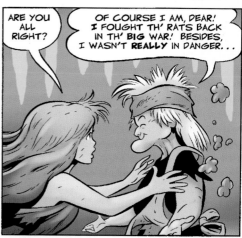

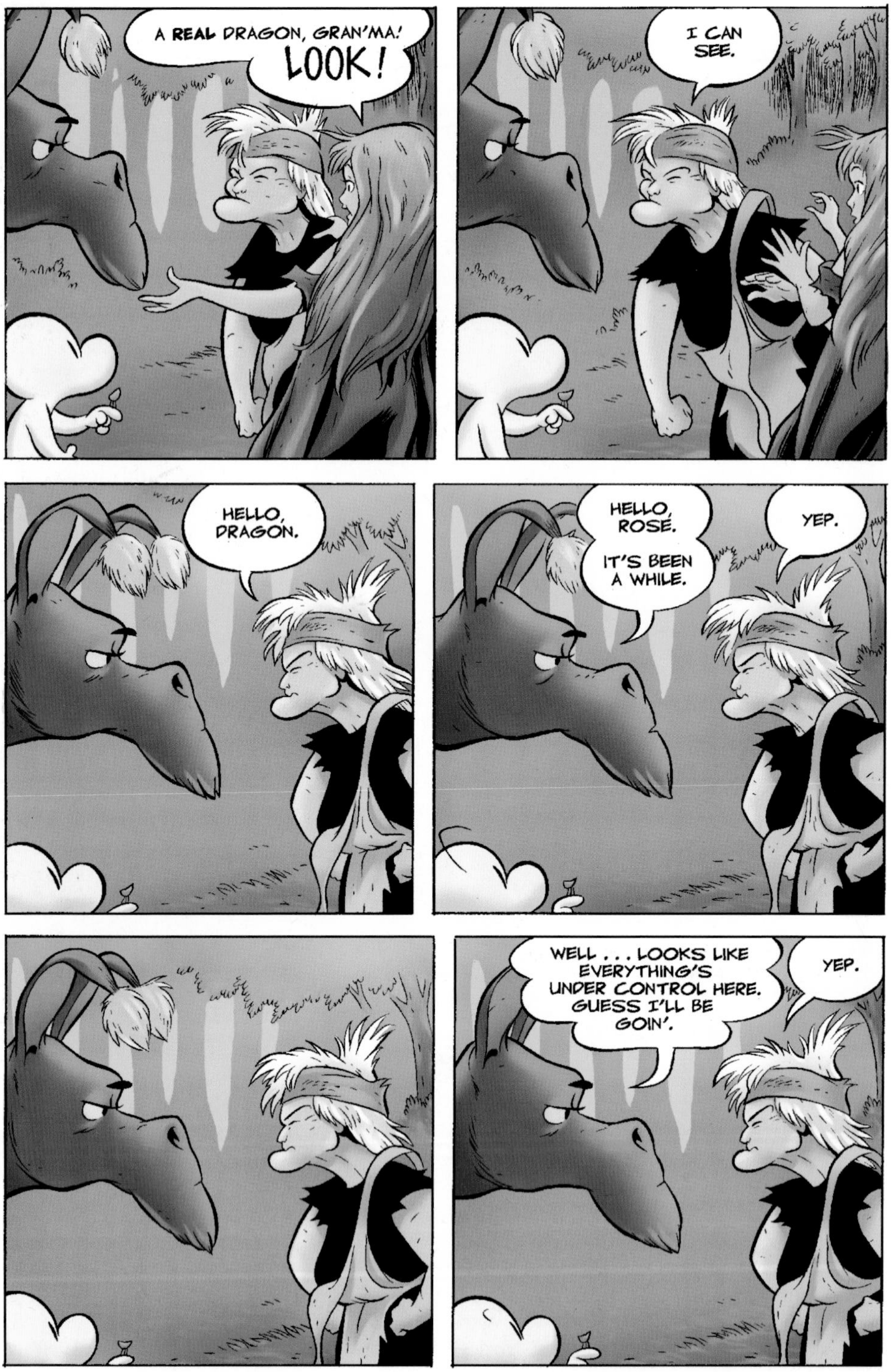
A REAL DRAGON, GRAN'MA!
LOOK!
I CAN SEE.
HELLO, DRAGON.
HELLO, ROSE.
IT'S BEEN A WHILE.
YEP.
WELL . . . LOOKS LIKE EVERYTHING'S UNDER CONTROL HERE. GUESS I'LL BE GOIN'.
YEP.

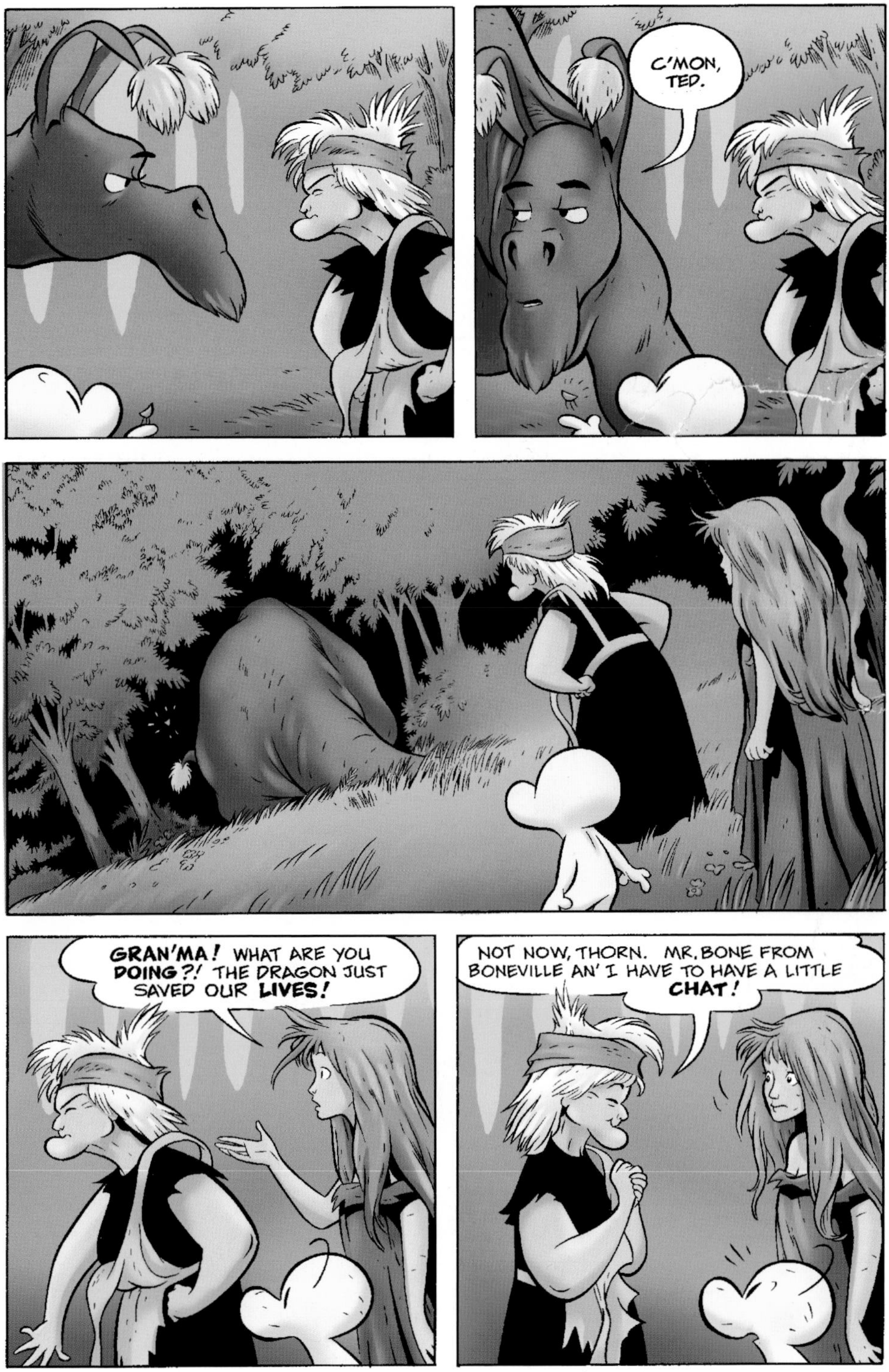
C'MON, TED.
GRAN'MA! WHAT ARE YOU DOING?! THE DRAGON JUST SAVED OUR LIVES!
NOT NOW, THORN. MR. BONE FROM BONEVILLE AN' I HAVE TO HAVE A LITTLE CHAT!

AND **YOU** HAVE A LOT OF THINGS TO DO BEFORE WE LEAVE FOR TH' **SPRING FAIR**!

THE **FAIR** ?! YOU'RE NOT STILL WORRIED ABOUT YOUR **COW RACE** ?!

WHAT ABOUT **PHONEY BONE** AN' **SMILEY** ? WE HAVE TO **FIND** THEM!

BONE AND I WILL HITCH UP TH' CART. **YOU** BE A SWEETHEART AND PUT OUT TH' **FIRE** ON TH' ROOF!

SHE'S NOT EVEN **LISTENING** TO US! CAN YOU **BELIEVE** SHE WANTS TO GO TO TH' **FAIR** ?!

ARE YOU **KIDDING** ? I STILL CAN'T GET OVER TH' FACT THAT SHE HAS A **FIRST NAME**!

DEAR ... I'M NOT A **COMPLETE** NINCOMPOOP! WE'LL BE **SAFER** IN TOWN! **AND**, WITH ANY LUCK, WE'LL BE ABLE TO FIND HIS **COUSINS**!

BUT --

PLEASE, THORN! WE **HAVE** TO GO! WE DON'T KNOW IF THEY'RE SAFE!

YOU'RE RIGHT! I'LL TAKE CARE OF THE ROOF!

WE PACKED EVERYTHING LAST NIGHT, SO TH' LUGGAGE IS ALREADY OUT IN TH' BARN. COME JOIN US WHEN YOU GET DONE.

C'MON, BONE!

GRAN'MA? WHAT **WAS** THAT WITH YOU AN' TH' DRAGON? DO YOU GUYS **KNOW** EACH OTHER?

I'LL ASK TH' QUESTIONS! I WANNA KNOW WHY THOSE MONSTERS WERE AFTER **YOU** ... AN' I WANT TH' **TRUTH**!

I HAVE **NO** IDEA! **HONEST**! I'VE NEVER DONE **ANYTHING** TO THEM!

WHAT ABOUT THAT SHIFTY **COUSIN** OF YOURS? YOU THINK **PHONEY BONE** MIGHT'VE HAD SOME DEALIN'S WITH 'EM?

NO, MA'M! WE DON'T **HAVE** RAT CREATURES BACK WHERE WE COME FROM!

IN FACT, WE NEVER EVEN **HEARD** OF RAT CREATURES BEFORE WE GOT RUN OUT OF BONEVILLE!

WELL, ACTUALLY, I WASN'T RUN OUTTA BONEVILLE -- **PHONEY** WAS! SMILEY AN' I JUST HELPED HIM GET AWAY!

WHAT'D HE **DO?**

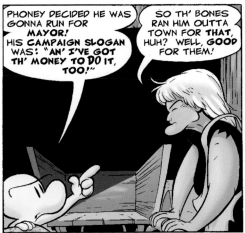

PHONEY DECIDED HE WAS GONNA RUN FOR **MAYOR!** HIS CAMPAIGN SLOGAN WAS: "AN' I'VE GOT TH' **MONEY** TO **DO** IT, TOO!"

SO TH' BONES RAN HIM OUTTA TOWN FOR **THAT**, HUH? WELL, **GOOD** FOR THEM!

NO. ANYBODY CAN RUN FOR MAYOR. EVEN **PHONEY!**

THAT GREEDY, LITTLE **LOUDMOUTH?** NOT IN MY TOWN HE COULDN'T!

WELL, HE CAN IN BONEVILLE. ANYWAY, HE WANTED TO MAKE THE **OFFICIAL** ANNOUNCEMENT A BIG **SOCIAL** EVENT, SO HE DECIDED TO THROW A PICNIC DOWN ON TH' BANKS OF TH' **ROLLING BONE** RIVER . . .

THERE'S A **BEAUTIFUL** PARK THERE WITH GREEN, SLOPING LAWNS THAT STRETCH TO THE EDGE OF TH' WATER. IT'S JUST FAR ENOUGH AWAY FROM TH' **HUSTLE** AN' **BUSTLE** OF DOWNTOWN BONEVILLE THAT THERE WOULDN'T BE ANY **DISTRACTIONS!**

PHONEY INVITED **EVERYBODY** IN TOWN -- AN' HE PROMISED **FREE FOOD** FOR ANYONE WHO SHOWED UP! PRETTY SOON, TH' **PICNIC** WAS TH' **TALK** OF **BONEVILLE!**

THEN TH' BIG DAY ARRIVED, AN' TH' **WHOLE TOWN** TURNED OUT! TH' KIDS WERE PLAYIN' UNDER TH' TREES, AN' THE WOMEN WORE SUNBONNETS AN' FANCY DRESSES! THE PICNIC WAS OFF TO A **PERFECT START!**

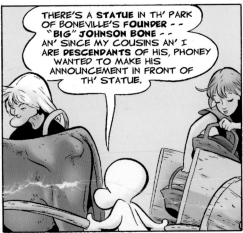

THERE'S A **STATUE** IN TH' PARK OF BONEVILLE'S **FOUNDER** -- "BIG" JOHNSON BONE -- AN' SINCE MY COUSINS AN' I ARE **DESCENDANTS** OF HIS, PHONEY WANTED TO MAKE HIS ANNOUNCEMENT IN FRONT OF TH' STATUE.

... AND JUST TO **ADD** TO TH' FESTIVITIES, PHONEY HAD A **50** ft. **BALLOON** MADE OF HIMSELF! TH' BALLOON WAS TIED TO OL' "**BIG**" JOHNSON!

FASTEN THAT END THERE, WOULD YOU, BONE?

EVERYTHING WAS GOIN' GREAT! FOLKS WERE LISTENIN' TO TH' **FIREHOUSE** BAND AN' ENJOYIN' TH' SUNSHINE! TH' FOOD WAS PASSED OUT AN' THERE WERE PLENTY OF **PRUNE TARTS** FOR **EVERYONE!**

PRUNE TARTS?

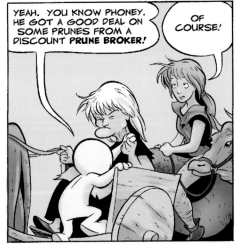

YEAH. YOU KNOW PHONEY. HE GOT A GOOD DEAL ON SOME PRUNES FROM A DISCOUNT **PRUNE BROKER!**

OF COURSE!

SO ANYWAY, HE MAKES THE **ANNOUNCEMENT**, RIGHT? HE GETS UP AND DECLARES HIS CANDIDACY FOR **MAYOR** OF **BONEVILLE**!

I STILL THINK **THAT'S** WHEN THEY SHOULD'VE RUN HIM OUT!

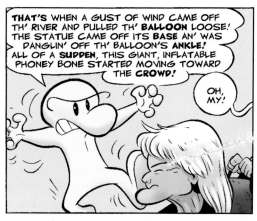

THAT'S WHEN A **GUST** OF WIND CAME OFF TH' RIVER AND PULLED TH' **BALLOON** LOOSE! THE STATUE CAME OFF ITS **BASE** AN' WAS DANGLIN' OFF TH' BALLOON'S **ANKLE**! ALL OF A **SUDDEN**, THIS GIANT, INFLATABLE PHONEY BONE STARTED MOVING TOWARD THE **CROWD**!

OH, MY!

YEAH, IT WAS **AMAZING**! MY FIRST-GRADE TEACHER, **MISS CRAB-BONE**, WAS THE FIRST TO **PANIC**! SHE STARTED SCREAMING AND RUNNING BACK AN' FORTH! THE BALLOON CHASED HER INTO TH' **RIVER** BEFORE SMILEY AND I COULD LET THE **AIR** OUT OF IT!

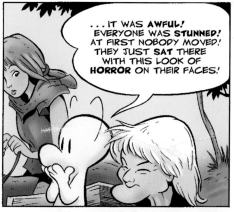

...IT WAS **AWFUL**! EVERYONE WAS **STUNNED**! AT FIRST NOBODY MOVED! THEY JUST **SAT** THERE WITH THIS LOOK OF **HORROR** ON THEIR FACES!

AN' **THAT'S** WHEN THEY RAN YOU OUTTA TOWN.

NO. THAT'S WHEN TH' **BAD PRUNES** KICKED IN...

...I JUST WANT YOU TO **KNOW**... I'VE BEEN **WORKING** ON **THE PLAN**! I BEEN SPREADIN' **RUMORS** ALL DAY THAT **GRAN'MA BEN** IS **TOO OLD** TO WIN TH' RACE THIS YEAR!

IS ANYBODY **BUYIN'** IT?

I'M TH' **BARTENDER**! THEY **GOTTA** BELIEVE ME!

THIS IS **TOO** **EASY**! WE'LL COVER ALL TH' **BETS**, AND THEN WHEN GRAN'MA **WINS**, WE'LL BE **RICH**!

OF COURSE, WHEN GRAN'MA GETS INTO **TOWN**, EVERYBODY'S GONNA SEE SHE'S **PERFECTLY FIT**!

I'VE GOT THAT COVERED WITH **PHASE TWO**:

THE MYSTERY COW!

A **COW** THAT WE'LL **BUILD UP** IN EVERYBODY'S IMAGINATION THAT **CAN'T BE BEAT**!

WAIT! IS **THAT** TH' PART WHERE I GET TO WEAR TH' **COW SUIT**?! OH, **JOY!**

YEAH, **THAT'S** TH' PART! BUT YOU'RE GONNA **THROW** TH' RACE! REMEMBER! WE **WANT** GRAN'MA BEN TO WIN!

WELL, **NATURALLY**, I'M LOOKING FORWARD TO WEARIN' A **COW** SUIT -- BUT WHAT DO **YOU** GET OUT OF IT? AFTER **ALL**, THE LOCALS DON'T USE **MONEY**! THEY TRADE GOODS 'N' SERVICES!

IT **DOES** SOUR MY PLANS FOR AMASSING A HUGE FORTUNE AND RETURNING TO BONEVILLE IN **TRIUMPH**... **STILL**, THE PLAY IS TH' THING!

IF ALL THESE YOKELS **HAVE** ARE **POULTRY PRODUCTS** THEN I'LL **TAKE IT!!**

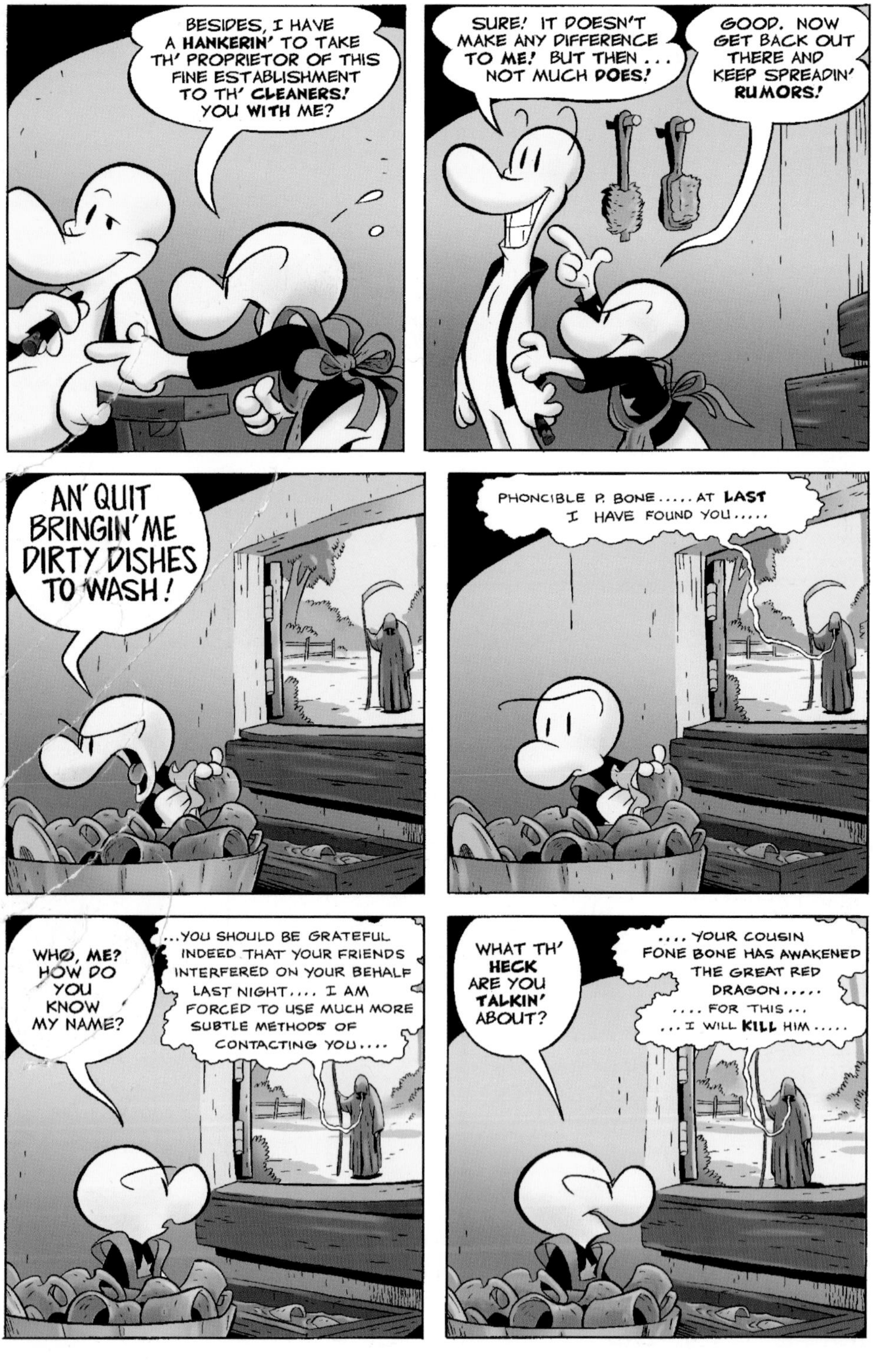
BESIDES, I HAVE A HANKERIN' TO TAKE TH' PROPRIETOR OF THIS FINE ESTABLISHMENT TO TH' CLEANERS! YOU WITH ME?
SURE! IT DOESN'T MAKE ANY DIFFERENCE TO ME! BUT THEN . . . NOT MUCH DOES!
GOOD. NOW GET BACK OUT THERE AND KEEP SPREADIN' RUMORS!
AN' QUIT BRINGIN' ME DIRTY DISHES TO WASH!
PHONCIBLE P. BONE . . . . . AT LAST I HAVE FOUND YOU . . . . .
WHO, ME? HOW DO YOU KNOW MY NAME?
. . . YOU SHOULD BE GRATEFUL INDEED THAT YOUR FRIENDS INTERFERED ON YOUR BEHALF LAST NIGHT . . . . I AM FORCED TO USE MUCH MORE SUBTLE METHODS OF CONTACTING YOU . . . .
WHAT TH' HECK ARE YOU TALKIN' ABOUT?
. . . . YOUR COUSIN FONE BONE HAS AWAKENED THE GREAT RED DRAGON . . . . .
. . . . FOR THIS . . .
. . . I WILL KILL HIM . . . . .

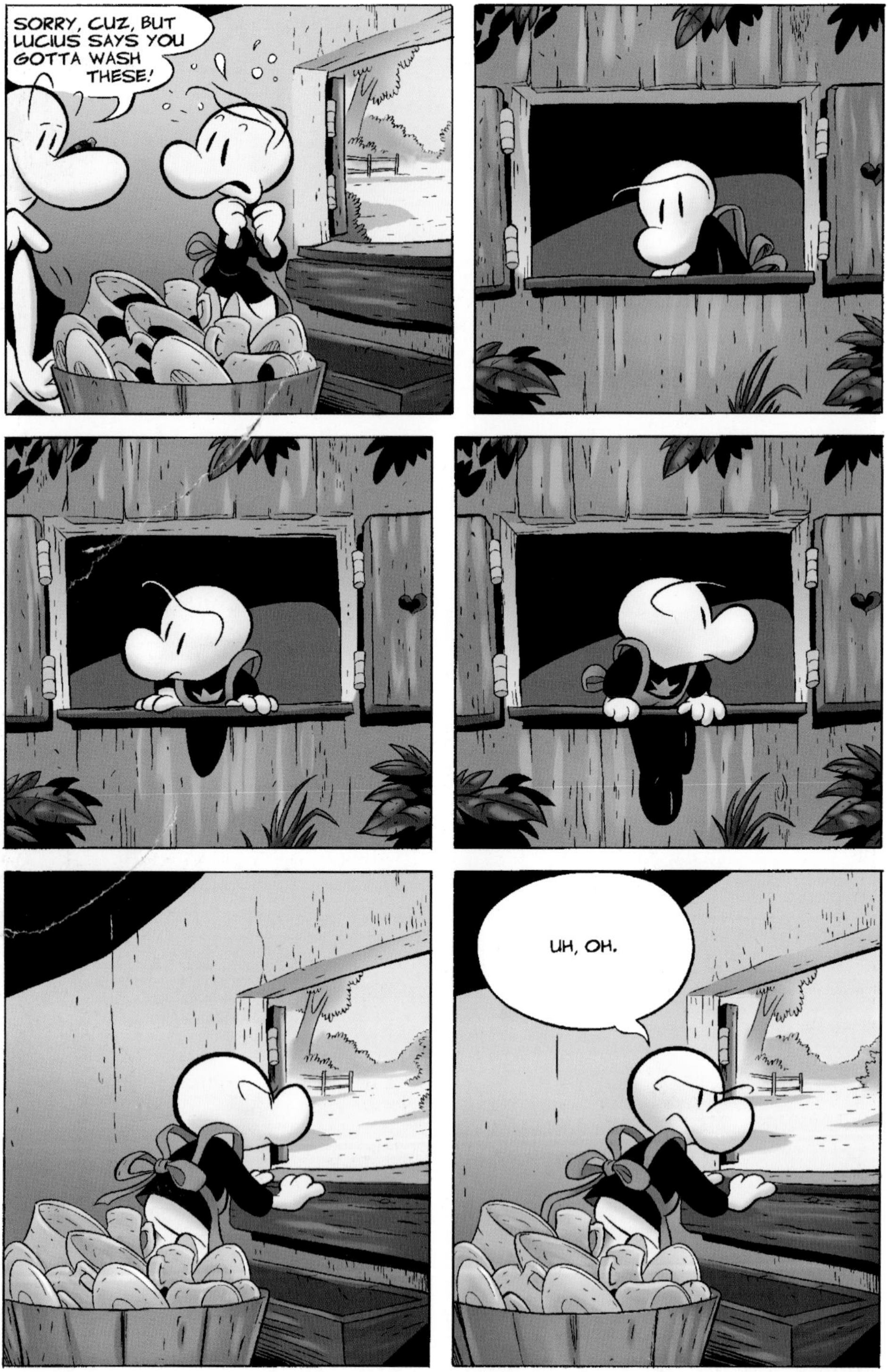
SORRY, CUZ, BUT LUCIUS SAYS YOU GOTTA WASH THESE!
UH, OH.

...SO THERE HE IS, OKAY? **ISHMAEL'S** LAYIN' IN HIS BUNK WAITIN' FOR HIS MYSTERIOUS NEW ROOMMATE TO SHOW UP ... **SUDDENLY** -- AT LIKE, **3 O' CLOCK** IN TH' MORNING -- TH' DOOR SWINGS **OPEN** ... AN' **THERE,** STANDIN' IN TH' DOORWAY, WITH TH' LIGHT FROM TH' HALL BEHIND HIM, IS **QUEEQUEG!** AN' HE'S **CARRYIN' SHRUNKEN HEADS !!**

WHAT'S GOING ON, BACK THERE?

OH ... H'LO, THORN.

ARE YOU TALKING ABOUT **MOBY DICK** **AGAIN?**

IT JUST SO HAPPENS THAT GRAN'MA **LIKES** TO HEAR ABOUT **GOOD BOOKS!** SHE **APPRECIATES** FINE LITERATURE!

HEY, GRAN'MA! WAKE UP!

ZZ--SNORT!

WHA -- ARE WE THERE ALREADY?

DOO-OOP!

NOT QUITE. BUT I THOUGHT I SHOULD WAKE YOU UP.

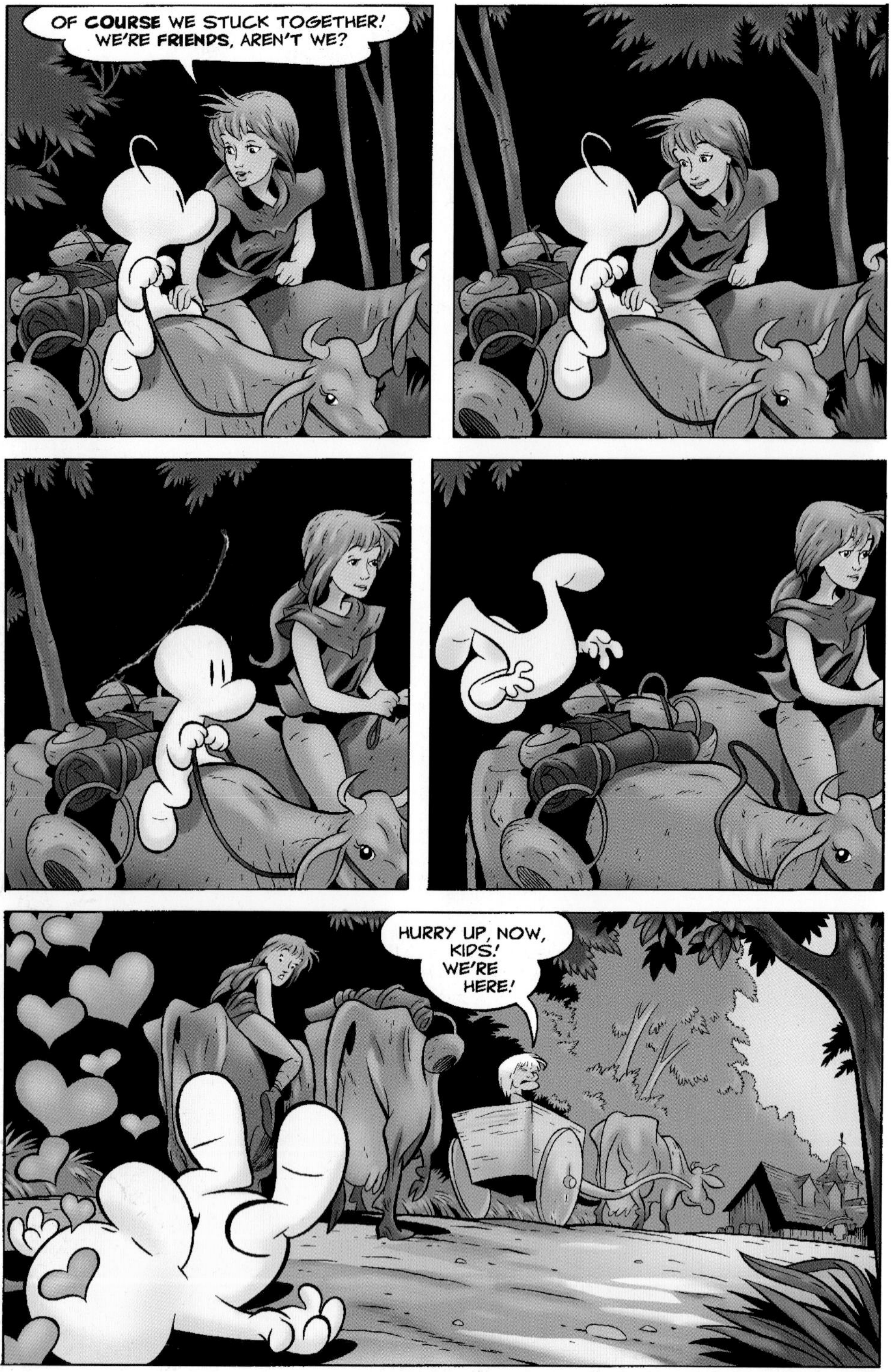
OF **COURSE** WE STUCK TOGETHER! WE'RE **FRIENDS**, AREN'T WE?
HURRY UP, NOW, KIDS! WE'RE HERE!

WELL, WELL . . . IT'S ABOUT **TIME**!

HELLO, LUCIUS!

HOW YA DOIN', ROSIE? WAS TH' **ROAD** SAFE? I WAS **WORRIED** ABOUT YA!

TH' ROAD WAS CLEAR . . . EXCEPT FOR YOUR **ROADBLOCK**!

OH! I GOT SOMETHIN' FOR YA! **HERE**! I BEEN SAVIN' IT IN MY POCKET ALL DAY!

OH, AREN'T YOU SWEET!

. . . WELLL . . . . . I HAD A LITTLE EXTRA **TIME** ON MY HANDS THIS MORNING . . .

. . . I GOT A COUPLE OF **DEADBEATS** INSIDE TAKIN' CARE OF TH' **CUSTOMERS** -- IN FACT, THEY LOOK A **LOT** LIKE THIS LITTLE FELLA YOU GOT HERE.

THEY **DO**?!

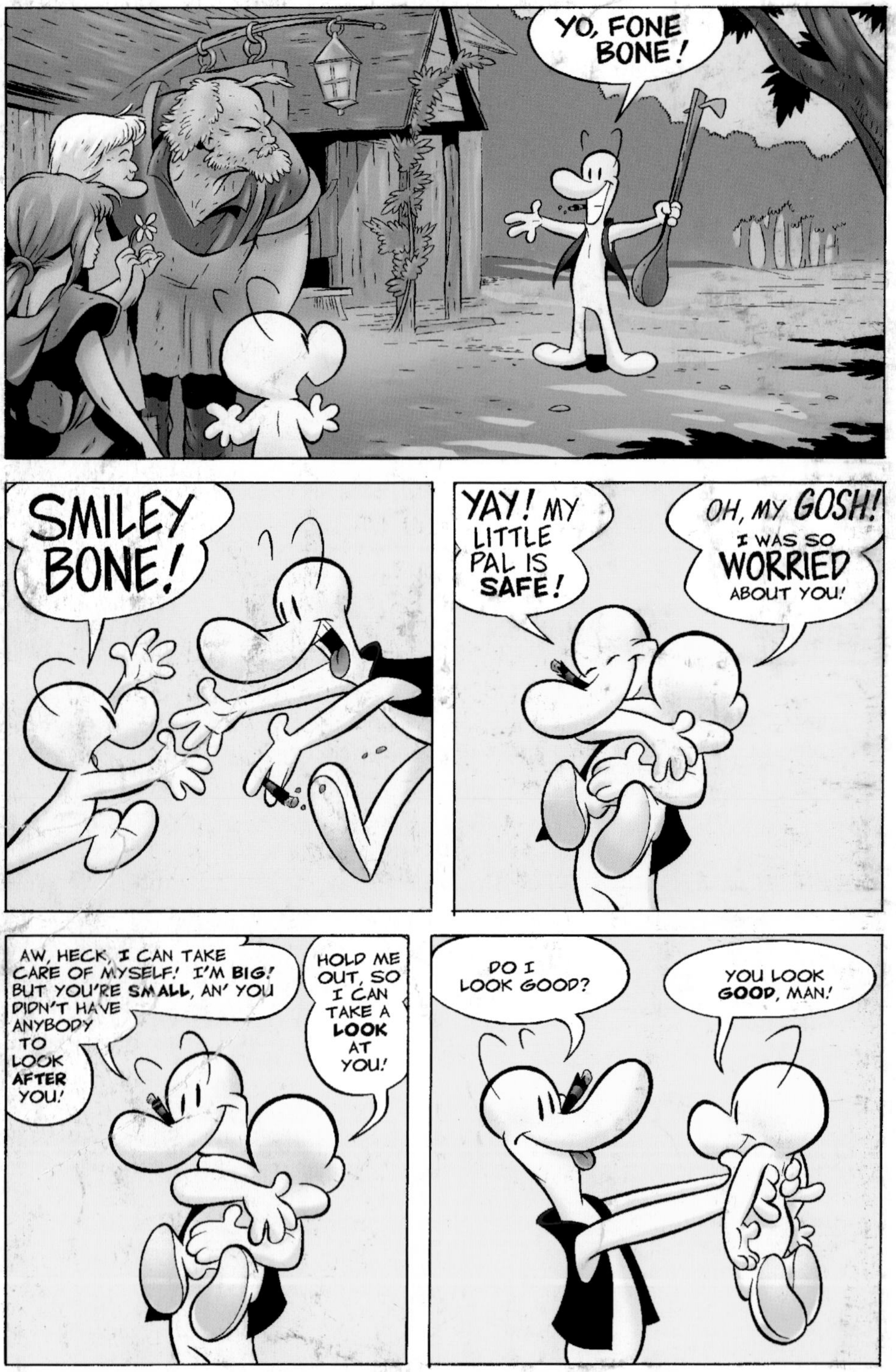
YO, FONE BONE!
SMILEY BONE!
YAY! MY LITTLE PAL IS SAFE!
OH, MY GOSH! I WAS SO WORRIED ABOUT YOU!
AW, HECK, I CAN TAKE CARE OF MYSELF! I'M BIG! BUT YOU'RE SMALL, AN' YOU DIDN'T HAVE ANYBODY TO LOOK AFTER YOU!
HOLD ME OUT, SO I CAN TAKE A LOOK AT YOU!
DO I LOOK GOOD?
YOU LOOK GOOD, MAN!

WHERE'S **PHONEY?**

HE'S RIGHT INSIDE! I'LL CALL HIM OUT!

NOW, JUST A MINUTE! I DON'T WANT **EVERYBODY** OUT HERE! WHO'LL TAKE CARE OF TH' **CUSTOMERS?**

LET 'EM GO, **LUCIUS!** THESE BOYS HAVEN'T BEEN TOGETHER FOR MONTHS!

THOSE BOYS OWE ME A LOTTA **EGGS,** ROSIE . . . .

OH, ALL RIGHT . . . **CALL** HIM OUT! BUT THEN GET **BACK TO WORK!**

THANKS, YA BIG LUG!

HEY, **PHONEY!** C'MON OUT! FONE BONE'S HERE!

About JEFF SMITH

JEFF SMITH was born and raised in the American Midwest. He learned about cartooning from comic strips, comic books, and watching animated shorts on TV. After four years of drawing comic strips for Ohio State University's student newspaper and cofounding Character Builders animation studio in 1986, Smith launched the comic book *BONE* in 1991. Between *BONE* and other comics projects, Smith spends much of his time on the international guest circuit promoting comics and the art of graphic novels.

More about *BONE*

Instant classics when they first appeared in the U.S. as underground comic books in 1991, the *BONE* books have since garnered 38 international awards and sold a million copies in 15 languages. Now, Scholastic's GRAPHIX imprint is publishing full-color graphic novel editions of the nine-book *BONE* series. Look for the continuing adventures of the Bone cousins in *The Great Cow Race*.